"Christin Ditchfield's love for children an
ents is evident in *A Family Guide to Narnia*. ‹
a light on God's truth, so we can all be bet
> —VICKI CARUANA, America's Teacher™,
> author of the best-selling books *Apples & Chalkdust* and
> *The Homeschooler's Guide*

"This is an important book that will help families learn more from the Bible and *The Chronicles of Narnia*."
> —LYLE W. DORSETT, Professor of Christian Ministries,
> Wheaton College

"*A Family Guide to Narnia* is the best (if not the only) detailed analysis of the biblical truths found in *The Chronicles of Narnia*. This cohesive and easy-to-follow guide serves as a fantastic parental teaching tool on a subject that kids love—the magical adventures of Aslan. Every child who loves Narnia needs to have a copy of this guide to help the stories of Aslan come alive in a biblically relevant way."
> —ELLIE KAY, Gold Medallion finalist and best-selling author
> of *Heroes at Home—Hope and Help for American*
> *Military Families*

"Christin has done a masterful job! This is a wonderful exploration of the biblical themes woven into *The Chronicles of Narnia*, with lively and help-ful introductions and an uncontrived use of Scripture throughout. I think it's ideal for families who want to study Lewis's classics at a deeper level."
> —PAUL MCCUSKER, Author of *Epiphany* and dramatist of
> *The Chronicles of Narnia Radio Theatre*

A FAMILY GUIDE TO

NARNIA

Biblical Truths in
C. S. LEWIS'S
The Chronicles of Narnia

Christin Ditchfield

CROSSWAY BOOKS

A PUBLISHING MINISTRY OF
GOOD NEWS PUBLISHERS
WHEATON, ILLINOIS

A Family Guide to Narnia

Copyright © 2003 by Christin Ditchfield

Published by Crossway Books
    a publishing ministry of Good News Publishers
    1300 Crescent Street
    Wheaton, Illinois 60187

Cover design: David LaPlaca

Cover photos: Getty Images

First printing, 2003

Printed in the United States of America

Scripture taken from the *Holy Bible: New International Version®*. Copyright © 1973, 1978, 1984 by International Bible Society. Used by permission of Zondervan Publishing House. All rights reserved.

The "NIV" and "New International Version" trademarks are registered in the United States Patent and Trademark Office by International Bible Society. Use of either trademark requires the permission of International Bible Society.

Scripture quotations marked ESV are taken from the English Standard Version, copyright © 2001 by Crossway Bibles, a publishing ministry of Good News Publishers.

Scripture quotations marked KJV are taken from the King James Version.

Library of Congress Cataloging-in-Publication Data
Ditchfield, Christin
   A family guide to Narnia : biblical truths in C.S. Lewis's Chronicles of
Narnia / Christin Ditchfield.
   p. cm.
   ISBN 1-58134-515-1 (TPB : alk. paper)
   1. Lewis, C.S. (Clive Staples), 1898-1963. Chronicles of Narnia.
2. Children's stories, English—History and criticism. 3. Christian fiction,
English—History and criticism. 4. Fantasy fiction, English—History and
criticism. 5. Narnia (Imaginary place). 6. Bible—In literature. I. Title.
PR6023.E926C5325   2003
823'.912—dc21   2003003724

ML		15	14	13	12	11	10	09	08	07	06
17	16	15	14	13	12	11	10	9	8	7	

This book is dedicated to
two special women who did so much to
encourage and inspire my lifelong love of reading.

AUNTIE DIANE,
who introduced me to many wonderful classics,
including *The Chronicles of Narnia*.

AUNTIE JACQUIE,
who was also my favorite elementary schoolteacher.
Years later, when I became a teacher myself, she invited me
to share *The Chronicles of Narnia* with her students.
From that experience, this book was born.

CONTENTS

FOREWORD

By Wayne Martindale

How many of us, after finishing a Narnia book (or any Lewis book), drop the volume to our laps and cast our eyes to the distance in wonder: Where did he get a vision of such cosmic sweep? How did he come to understand such depths of human longing? How could he know so much about the complex mix of good and evil, both in the world at large and in each human heart? What accounts for the energy and the urgency? Why do these books reach me at such depths of hope and fear? The most important answer to each of these questions is: the Bible. Jesus had Lewis's heart, and Lewis's head was filled with biblical knowledge.

To be sure, there have been few as profoundly learned in the languages, literature, history, and philosophy of the entire human race, but all this learning he interpreted through the lens of Scripture. Christin Ditchfield's *A Family Guide to Narnia* richly illustrates how true this is as she displays chapter by chapter how each book in the seven-volume *Chronicles of Narnia* teems with biblical parallels and insights. No matter how many times we read these books, there always seems to be something new to discover.

A friend once quipped that one of the best things about being a parent is having an excuse for reading the Narnia books all over again. Whether you are reading the books to the children in your life or just have the haunting feeling there is more here but you can't quite put your finger on it, *A Family Guide to Narnia* will help you glean the wealth of biblical background and make applications to life.

Lewis had what could be called a biblical imagination. The truths about God—about God's plan for human history, the realms of good and evil, and the ethics that flow from an understanding of God's character—all of this and more informs everything he wrote. In writing these stories, Lewis wasn't allegorizing Scripture, however. As he says, "With me all fiction *begins with* pictures in my head"—some that had been there since he was sixteen. But as he spun the tales, because his mind was so thoroughly suffused with Scripture, he wrote, second nature, stories of profound theological heft. It was simply part of who he was and how his mind worked. In this sense, Lewis worked from the Bible to the stories; Ditchfield's *Guide* works from the stories back to the Bible. Working through the *Guide* will not only enhance our understanding and appreciation of the Narnia books but will educate us in the scope of the Bible and its relevance to everyday life.

A guide of this substance and clarity could only have been written by someone with a rich and thorough knowledge of both Lewis's work (and not just the *Chronicles*) and the Bible. As Christin Ditchfield shows, Lewis's Bible knowledge ranges from Genesis to Revelation. What arrested me in reading through this *Guide* for the first time was how important the Old Testament is to both the background of Narnia and to issues of contemporary life.

Lewis took seriously the Bible's command to bring "every thought captive to . . . Christ." Ditchfield's guide is a valuable aid in helping us do the same. If you've been looking for a way to jump-start private or family devotions, your search may be over.

Wayne Martindale
Professor of English
Wheaton College

PREFACE

I was seven years old when I was given my first copy of *The Lion, the Witch and the Wardrobe*. Little did I know that it would have a profound and lasting impact on my life. I quickly devoured the entire Narnia series. Over the next few years I read each of the books more than a dozen times, until they literally fell apart. Every time I read them, I enjoyed them more. And I discovered, as millions of others have, that there is far more to *The Chronicles of Narnia* than meets the eye. There are stories within the stories. *The Chronicles of Narnia* are full of hidden truths, deep mysteries, and spiritual treasures.

C.S. Lewis insisted that *The Chronicles* are not allegories, though many people have described them as such. Technically speaking, this is true. In an allegory, every character and event is a symbol of something else. Many of the characters and events in Narnia do not represent anything in particular— they are simply elements of the wonderful and fantastic adventures Lewis created. But many characters and events *do* represent something else, something from the spiritual realm. And although Lewis did not initially intend to write stories that would illustrate the most vital truths of the Christian faith, that is essentially what he did.

Jesus said, "Out of the abundance of the heart the mouth speaks" (Matthew 12:34, ESV). Consciously and perhaps at times even unconsciously, Lewis wound powerful biblical truths through every chapter, every scene in *The Chronicles*. His deeply rooted faith naturally found its expression in everything he wrote.

In *The Voyage of the Dawn Treader* (Book 5), the great Lion Aslan tells the two Pevensie children that their adventures in Narnia have come to an end. They will not be returning to this country again. Edmund and Lucy are horribly upset.

"It isn't Narnia, you know," sobbed Lucy. "It's you. We shan't meet you there. And how can we live, never meeting you?"

"But you shall meet me, dear one," said Aslan.

"Are—are you there too, Sir?" said Edmund.

"I am," said Aslan. "But there I have another name. You must learn to know me by that name. This was the very reason why you were brought to Narnia, that by knowing me here for a little, you may know me better there."

Years ago, after reading this passage in *Dawn Treader*, a little girl named Hila wrote to C.S. Lewis, asking him to tell her Aslan's other name. Lewis responded, "Well, I want you to guess. Has there ever been anyone in this world who 1) arrived at the same time as Father Christmas, 2) Said he was the son of the Great Emperor, 3) Gave himself up for someone else's fault to be jeered at and killed by wicked people, 4) Came to life again, 5) Is sometimes spoken of as a lamb (see the end of *Dawn Treader*). Don't you really know His name in this world? Think it over and let me know your answer."

Edmund and Lucy's adventures in Narnia helped them come to know Aslan (Jesus) better, and our adventures in Narnia can do the same for us. But sometimes, like little Hila, we may miss the deeper truths behind the stories. This book is written to help readers identify and understand some of the many spiritual treasures in *The Chronicles of Narnia*. It is meant to be read side by side with the original books.

For each chapter in each book of *The Chronicles*, you will find a key verse that reflects one of the primary spiritual themes of the chapter. You'll also find a list of biblical parallels and principles. In some cases this section shows which events in Narnia are similar—or even identical—to stories in the Bible. In other cases it indicates where a particular element of Lewis's story illustrates an important scriptural principle. The chapter concludes with an interesting fact or point to ponder and some additional Scriptures you can read, related to a previously mentioned topic.

Parents, grandparents, and teachers who are reading along with their children may want to use the material in this book to help start discussion or even extend story time into Scripture reading and family devotions. If you plan to use the book this way, it would be best not to attempt to cover all of the material offered in each and every chapter. Instead, choose one or two points that seem most interesting or meaningful to you, and go from there.

Preface

It is my hope and prayer that this book will help those who want to gain a deeper understanding and appreciation of *The Chronicles of Narnia*, and that having read this book, you will love the original series all the more. Ultimately may you find yourself developing an even deeper love for the source of Lewis's inspiration: the Word of God.

Christin Ditchfield

THE
MAGICIAN'S
NEPHEW

Introduction to

The Magician's Nephew

In the opening paragraph of *The Magician's Nephew*, we learn that we are about to read an "important" story—important because it shows "how all the comings and goings between our world and the land of Narnia first began." After writing five other books about Narnia, C.S. Lewis decided to go back and tell readers the story of Narnia's creation. (On Lewis's suggestion, publishers later renumbered the series, and *The Magician's Nephew* became Book One.)

When Uncle Andrew—the magician—tricks his nephew Digory and neighbor girl Polly into trying on his magic rings, the children discover that there are countless worlds beyond our own. They first visit Charn—an ancient world in ruin and decay, destroyed by the wickedness and corruption of its people. The last survivor of Charn, and the one ultimately responsible for its destruction, is Jadis. (This wicked Queen later becomes the White Witch in *The Lion, the Witch and the Wardrobe*.) Jadis grabs onto Digory and follows the children back to our world, where she begins to wreak havoc on the city of London. In an attempt to return her to Charn, the children accidentally stumble into Narnia—just as Aslan is singing it into existence. They are eyewitnesses to the miraculous creation of a glorious new world. But Narnia's beauty and perfection is marred almost immediately by the presence of Jadis, whom Digory has unwittingly brought along. Unable to bear being in the presence of the great Lion, Jadis flees to the North. She will return to threaten Narnia in the future.

The story of *The Magician's Nephew* is essentially the story of Creation and the fall of Man. Digory is responsible for bringing evil (Jadis) into Narnia. "Sin entered the world through one man, and death through sin" (Romans 5:12). As Aslan prophesies, "Evil will come of that evil, but it is still a long way off, and I will see to it that the worst falls upon myself. . . . And as Adam's race has done the harm, Adam's race shall help heal it." This foreshadows the story of *The Lion, the Witch and the Wardrobe*—just as God's promise to Adam and Eve in Genesis 3:15 foreshadows the defeat of Satan at the cross, where Jesus destroyed the power of sin and death by sacrificing His own life for ours.

Power is a central theme in *The Magician's Nephew*—the power of pride, the power of temptation, the power of sin, the power of evil. Jadis, like Satan, is thoroughly corrupted by a lust for power and dominion over others. Uncle Andrew has devoted his entire life to acquiring secret knowledge and mysterious power through "scientific" experiments with the occult. Even Digory is tempted by a desire for power, though his motive is good: He wants the power to save his dying mother. In the end, it is only by refusing to grasp for power—and instead obeying Aslan's command—that Digory *and* his mother are saved.

Digory discovers the power of faith, the power of trust—the power that comes from obedience and submission to the will of God. "When I am weak, then I am strong" (2 Corinthians 12:10). *The Magician's Nephew* also includes illustrations of the following truths: "The man without the Spirit does not accept the things that come from the Spirit of God, for they are foolishness to him, and he cannot understand them" (1 Corinthians 2:14). "A friend loves at all times" (Proverbs 17:17). "As a father has compassion on his children, so the LORD has compassion on those who fear him" (Psalm 103:13).

These lessons are just a few of the spiritual treasures you will discover as you witness the creation of Narnia along with *The Magician's Nephew*.

1. THE WRONG DOOR

In his arrogance the wicked man hunts down the weak, who are caught in the schemes he devises. PSALM 10:2

Biblical Parallels and Principles

✢ The two children share an active imagination and a love for mystery and adventure. The Bible encourages believers to seek out hidden truths and spiritual treasures: "It is the glory of God to conceal a matter; to search out a matter is the glory of kings" (Proverbs 25:2).

✢ For a while, it seems, Uncle Andrew has been trying to get hold of Digory. This time the two children are caught unawares. Describing the ways of the wicked, Psalm 56:6 says, "They conspire, they lurk, they watch my steps." So the psalmist prays, "Keep me from the snares they have laid for me, from the traps set by evildoers" (Psalm 141:9). In Matthew 24:4 Jesus told His disciples, "Watch out that no one deceives you."

✢ Polly's alarm evaporates when Uncle Andrew compliments her. She lets down her guard and walks right into his trap. The psalmist observed, "The godly are no more. . . . Everyone lies to his neighbor; their flattering lips speak with deception" (Psalm 12:1-2). Romans 16:18 explains, "By smooth talk and flattery, they deceive the minds of naive people."

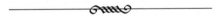

Do You Know?

Digory says that his uncle has "awful eyes." It's the eager, greedy look on Uncle Andrew's face that alerts Digory to the danger of the rings. Do you know what the Bible compares a person's eyes to?

(Hint: Read Matthew 6:22-23.)

Scriptures on Staying Alert

1 Peter 5:8-9   1 Corinthians 16:13-14   Ephesians 5:15-16

2. DIGORY AND HIS UNCLE

The righteous detest the dishonest; the wicked detest the upright.

PROVERBS 29:27

Biblical Parallels and Principles

❧ Uncle Andrew prides himself on his superior intellect. He believes that he is above the law—that the rules don't apply to him. Isaiah 5:21 warns, "Woe to those who are wise in their own eyes and clever in their own sight." Psalm 119:118 tells us that God rejects those who stray from His decrees. And Proverbs 28:9 says, "If anyone turns a deaf ear to the law, even his prayers are detestable."

❧ The magician is obsessed with obtaining secret knowledge. (Clearly it is not godly wisdom he seeks—he acquires this knowledge from "devilish" people in dark, dangerous places.) First Timothy 4:1 tells us that some people "follow deceiving spirits and things taught by demons." Revelation 2:24 speaks scathingly of those who claim to have learned "Satan's so-called deep secrets." First Corinthians 3:19 says, "The wisdom of this world is foolishness in God's sight." And James 3:15 explains, "Such 'wisdom' does not come down from heaven but is earthly, unspiritual, of the devil."

❧ Uncle Andrew praises the wicked and immoral, while mocking those who are decent and upright. Describing a wicked man, Psalm 10:3 observes, "He boasts of the cravings of his heart; he blesses the greedy and reviles the LORD." Isaiah 5:20 warns, "Woe to those who call evil good and good evil, who put darkness for light and light for darkness." God's anger will burn against them, and they will be destroyed (Isaiah 5:25).

❧ Digory is horrified by Uncle Andrew's complete disregard for the fate of the guinea pigs—and his total lack of concern for Polly's welfare. Proverbs 12:10 says, "The kindest acts of the wicked are cruel." Psalm 119:70 explains, "Their hearts are callous and unfeeling."

Think About It!

Digory tells his uncle, "You're simply a wicked, cruel magician like the ones in the stories. Well, I've never read a story in which people of that sort weren't paid out in the end." According to the Bible, what is the ultimate end of men like Uncle Andrew?

(Hint: Read Revelation 21:8.)

Scriptures on Loving Others As We Love Ourselves

Mark 12:28-31   1 Corinthians 13:1-8   1 John 4:7-11

3. THE WOOD BETWEEN THE WORLDS

He who trusts in himself is a fool, but he who walks in wisdom is kept safe. PROVERBS 28:26

Biblical Parallels and Principles

 Uncle Andrew's fascination with evil magic—or the occult—has led him to experiment with powers that are beyond his ability to understand or control. Ecclesiastes 8:8 warns, "No man has power over the wind to contain it . . . wickedness will not release those who practice it." Ephesians 6:12 makes it clear that supernatural powers do exist. Believers must be alert and on guard against "the powers of this dark world . . . the spiritual forces of evil in the heavenly realms."

 Polly and Digory are horrified to realize how close they have come to making a very foolish mistake. Throughout *The Chronicles*, in the midst of the most fantastic adventures, C.S. Lewis often reminds readers of the importance of "keeping your head." This theme is repeated in the Scriptures as well. Isaiah 44:19 laments, "No one stops to think." Haggai 1:7 urges, "Give careful thought to your ways." And Ephesians 5:15 warns God's people, "Be very careful, then, how you live—not as unwise but as wise, because the days are evil."

Do You Know?

Unlike Uncle Andrew, Digory has a *healthy* curiosity—a thirst for knowledge and a love of learning that will serve him well later on in life. (As Professor Kirke, he shares some of his wisdom and insight with the Pevensie children in *The Lion, the Witch and the Wardrobe*.) What does the Bible say about the value of godly wisdom?

(Hint: Read Proverbs 3:13-15.)

Scriptures on Searching for Wisdom and Knowledge

Proverbs 2:1-6   Isaiah 33:5-6   Job 32:6-9

4. THE BELL AND THE HAMMER

Like a city whose walls are broken down is a man who lacks self-control. PROVERBS 25:28

Biblical Parallels and Principles

❧ Notice how quickly Digory's healthy curiosity becomes unhealthy, when he allows it to control him. He becomes thoughtless, cruel, and selfish—just like Uncle Andrew! "A wise man fears the LORD and shuns evil, but a fool is hotheaded and reckless" (Proverbs 14:16). First Peter 4:7 urges believers to be "clear minded and self-controlled." And 2 Chronicles 19:6 says, "Consider carefully what you do."

❧ Digory says he can't help himself—he blames the Magic. But James 1:13-15 makes it clear that we cannot blame anyone or anything for our mistakes. We are responsible for our own choices: "Each one is tempted when, by his own evil desire, he is dragged away and enticed. Then, after desire has conceived, it gives birth to sin; and sin, when it is full-grown, gives birth to death."

Think About It!

Neither Polly nor Digory wants to be accused of being afraid—of *anything.* Each is determined to put on a brave face and plunge ahead, even when his or her better judgment tells him or her that caution is called for. How does the Bible say wise people respond to danger?

(Hint: Read Proverbs 22:3.)

Scriptures on Avoiding and Resisting Temptation

Proverbs 4:13-15   Romans 6:12-13   1 Corinthians 10:13

5. THE DEPLORABLE WORD

The memory of the righteous will be a blessing, but the name of the wicked will rot. PROVERBS 10:7

Biblical Parallels and Principles

ॐ Digory realizes that although they come from different worlds, Uncle Andrew and Jadis have the same spirit. Speaking of such people, Romans 1:29-31 says, "They have become filled with every kind of wickedness, evil, greed and depravity. They are full of envy, murder, strife, deceit and malice . . . God-haters, insolent, arrogant and boastful; they invent ways of doing evil . . . they are senseless, faithless, heartless, ruthless."

ॐ Charn gives us a horrific picture of the end result of unrestrained wickedness—the complete and total destruction of an entire civilization. The Bible tells us that our world will come to a similar end. In Matthew 24:6-7, 29, Jesus said, "You will hear of wars and rumors of wars. . . . Nation will rise against nation, and kingdom against kingdom . . . 'the sun will be darkened, and the moon will not give its light.'" There will be plagues, famines, floods, and earthquakes (Matthew 24:7; Revelation 16). Blood will flow in the streets (Revelation 14:20). But unlike Charn, our story will have a happy ending. God promises to rescue those who are His— He will create a new Heaven and a new earth for all who are faithful to Him (Revelation 21:1-4).

Sound Familiar?

Readers in C.S. Lewis's day saw an immediate connection between "the deplorable word" and the newly developed atom bomb. But Lewis did not view nuclear war as the ultimate threat to modern civilization. (In fact, he predicted that biological warfare might one day supersede it.) "As a Christian, I take it for granted that human history will some day end," Lewis said (*God in the Dock*, 1958.) The fall of Charn shows that the ultimate threat—whatever it is—is born out of the depravity of the human heart.

Scriptures on the Destiny of the Wicked

Philippians 3:18-19   2 Thessalonians 1:9   Psalm 37

6. THE BEGINNING OF UNCLE ANDREW'S TROUBLES

The look on their faces testifies against them; they parade their sin . . . they do not hide it. Woe to them! They have brought disaster upon themselves. ISAIAH 3:9

Biblical Parallels and Principles

🔖 Digory's misplaced sympathy allows Jadis to escape the Wood and follow the children into our world. Speaking of the wicked, Deuteronomy 7:16 says, "Do not look on them with pity . . . for that will be a snare to you." Ecclesiastes 7:26 warns about "the woman who is a snare, whose heart is a trap and whose hands are chains." Ephesians 4:27 cautions believers to guard their hearts against evil: "Do not give the devil a foothold." In Exodus 22:18 God tells His people in that day, "Do not allow a sorceress to live."

🔖 Jadis treats others as pawns in her quest for power. The psalmist prayed for protection from people like the Queen: "Rescue me, O LORD, from evil men; protect me from men of violence, who devise evil plans in their hearts and stir up war every day. They make their tongues as sharp as a serpent's; the poison of vipers is on their lips" (Psalm 140:1-3).

🔖 It's important that Polly and Digory make things right and repair their friendship. Ephesians 4:26-27 tells us not to let the sun go down on our anger. And Colossians 3:13 reminds us to "bear with each other and forgive whatever grievances you may have against one another. Forgive as the Lord forgave you."

Do You Know?

After a few "nasty grown-up drinks," Uncle Andrew begins to lose touch with reality. He forgets his initial—and very rational—fear of Jadis and imagines himself as the object of her desire. What does the Bible say alcohol will do to those who abuse it?

(Hint: Read Proverbs 23:29-35.)

Scriptures on Steering Clear of the Wicked

2 Timothy 3:1-5   Ephesians 5:11-12   1 Corinthians 15:33

7. WHAT HAPPENED AT THE FRONT DOOR

They sow the wind and reap the whirlwind. HOSEA 8:7

Biblical Parallels and Principles

❧ Aunt Letty mistakes Jadis—with her bare arms—for a circus performer. (At that time, the costumes worn by those in the entertainment industry were often considered immodest by "decent" people.) Though society's standards change from year to year and culture to culture, the Scripture says, "Women should adorn themselves in respectable apparel, with modesty and self-control, not with braided hair and gold or pearls or costly attire, but with what is proper for women who profess godliness— good works" (1 Timothy 2:9-10, ESV).

❧ Back in his study, Uncle Andrew had boasted of his wisdom and knowledge and power. No *ordinary* man, he claimed he was called to greatness— a "high and lonely destiny" (see Chapter Two). Staggering out of the ruins of the hansom, he presents quite a different picture. Proverbs 21:29 tells us, "A wicked man puts up a bold front." But "pride goes before destruction, a haughty spirit before a fall" (Proverbs 16:18). Hosea 10:13 observes, "You have planted wickedness, you have reaped evil."

Sound Familiar?

The Bible tells us that Israel was once ruled by a wicked and bloodthirsty queen. Like Jadis, her name also started with a J. Do you remember what it was?

(Hint: Read 1 Kings 18:1-4, 19, 40 and 19:1-2. For more about her, see 1 Kings 21:1-23.)

Scriptures on Reaping What You Sow

Proverbs 22:8   Galatians 6:7-9   Hosea 10:12

8. THE FIGHT AT THE LAMP-POST

Where were you when I laid the earth's foundation . . . while the morning stars sang together and all the angels shouted for joy? JOB 38:4, 7

Biblical Parallels and Principles

Polly, Digory, and the others begin to realize that they are witnessing the birth of a new world. Compare this scene to the account of Creation in Genesis 1:1-10, 14-19. "Now the earth was formless and empty, darkness was over the surface of the deep, and the Spirit of God was hovering over the waters. And God said, 'Let there be light,' and there was light" (vv. 2-3).

In *The Magician's Nephew* we learn that Aslan is not only Narnia's savior (as in *The Lion, the Witch and the Wardrobe*), but also its creator. The Bible tells us that although Jesus came to Earth just over two thousand years ago, He existed "before the world began" (John 17:5). Colossians 1:15-16 tells us Jesus is "the image of the invisible God, the firstborn over all creation. For by him all things were created: things in heaven and on earth, visible and invisible, whether thrones or powers or rulers or authorities; all things were created by him and for him." (See also John 1:1-3; 1 Corinthians 8:6; Ephesians 3:9; and Hebrews 1:1-2.)

To the children and the Cabby, Aslan's voice is beautiful. But Uncle Andrew and Jadis can't stand the sound of it. Romans 8:7 tells us, "The sinful mind is hostile to God. It does not submit to God, nor can it do so." John 3:20 explains, "Everyone who does evil hates the light, and will not come into the light for fear that his deeds will be exposed."

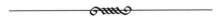

Do You Know?

Aslan sings to bring Narnia into existence. The Bible tells us that God also sings. Do you know why?

(Hint: Read Zephaniah 3:17.)

Scriptures on Singing

Psalm 95:1-7   Ephesians 5:19-20   Revelation 5:11-13

9. THE FOUNDING OF NARNIA

God saw all that he had made, and it was very good.

GENESIS 1:31

Biblical Parallels and Principles

 Aslan continues his creation of Narnia. Compare this scene to Genesis 1:9-11, 20-25, and 2:19. "Let the earth bring forth living creatures . . ."(Genesis 1:24, ESV). There are also elements that are very similar to the story of Noah in Genesis 6—7: "You are to bring into the ark two of all living creatures, male and female . . ." (Genesis 6:19). These animals were specially chosen to repopulate the earth after the Flood.

 Aslan breathes on the animals and gives them the gift of speech: "Be Talking Beasts." In Genesis 2:7 we read that God created Adam and "breathed into his nostrils the breath of life." And in John 20:22, Jesus breathed on His disciples and said, "Receive the Holy Spirit."

 Then "there came a swift flash like fire . . . either from the sky or from the Lion itself." This imagery is similar to that of Acts 2:2-4, where Jesus' disciples receive the Holy Spirit He had promised in John 20:22: "Suddenly a sound like the blowing of a violent wind came from heaven. . . . They saw what seemed to be tongues of fire that . . . came to rest on each of them. All of them were filled with the Holy Spirit and began to speak in other tongues. . . ."

Do You Know?

As he witnesses the spectacular creation of a wonderful new world, all Uncle Andrew can think about is how he may be able to profit from it. What does the Bible say about those who love money?

(Hint: Read Ecclesiastes 5:10 and 1 Timothy 6:9-10.)

Scriptures on the Wonders of Creation

Psalm 8:3-9   Psalm 19:1-6   Psalm 148

10. THE FIRST JOKE AND OTHER MATTERS

Our mouths were filled with laughter, our tongues with songs of joy. . . . PSALM 126:2

Biblical Parallels and Principles

✣ Aslan warns the Talking Beasts not to return to the ways of the Dumb Beasts or they will cease to be Talking Beasts: "For out of them you were taken and into them you can return." God told Adam that death was the ultimate result of his disobedience: "For dust you are and to dust you will return" (Genesis 3:19). Scripture tells us that many of God's blessings are conditional—they depend on our obedience and faithfulness to His commands (see Deuteronomy 30:15-20).

✣ When the animals speak, Uncle Andrew hears nothing but growling. Describing people like him, Ephesians 4:18 says, "They are darkened in their understanding and separated from the life of God because of the ignorance that is in them due to the hardening of their hearts." First Corinthians 2:14 says, "The man without the Spirit does not accept the things that come from the Spirit of God, for they are foolishness to him, and he cannot understand them, because they are spiritually discerned."

Think About It!

The Narnian creatures include fauns, satyrs, dwarfs, nymphs, and "gods and goddesses" of the wood and the river. These "gods" are not like those of Greek mythology—powerful, independent deities. In *The Chronicles* these "gods" are more like elves or fairies—supernatural beings, but subject to their Creator. In our world, they would be similar to angels.

Scriptures on Spiritual Blindness

Isaiah 44:18   Romans 1:18-25   Ephesians 4:17-24

11. DIGORY AND HIS UNCLE ARE BOTH IN TROUBLE

Sin entered the world through one man, and death through sin.

ROMANS 5:12

Biblical Parallels and Principles

❧ At first Digory refers to the Witch's arrival in Narnia as an accident. Then he tries to blame Uncle Andrew or the enchantment. Aslan's penetrating questions force him to confront the truth, confess his sin, and take responsibility for his actions. In Genesis 3:8-13, God questions Adam and Eve about eating the forbidden fruit: "What is this you have done?" At first they try to shift the blame to someone or something else. In the end, they are forced to face the truth and accept responsibility for their sin.

❧ Digory may have brought evil into Narnia, but he didn't create it. The wicked Queen comes from another world much older than Narnia or our own. The Bible tells us that the devil was once an angel who led a rebellion against God and was cast out of Heaven—long before our world was created (Isaiah 14:12-15; Luke 10:18). He first appeared on earth as the serpent in the Garden of Eden, where it seemed he successfully sabotaged God's beautiful new creation. But right from the start God made it clear that He would have the final word (Genesis 3:15; John 1:14; 1 John 3:8).

❧ Aslan says, "Evil will come of that evil, but it is still a long way off, and I will see to it that the worst falls upon myself. . . . And as Adam's race has done the harm, Adam's race shall help heal it." (That story is told in *The Lion, the Witch and the Wardrobe*.) In Genesis 3:15 God promised that He would one day crush the serpent: A descendant of Adam would bring about his defeat. This prophecy was fulfilled by Jesus. "He is the atoning sacrifice for our sins, and not only for ours but also for the sins of the whole world" (1 John 2:2). At the cross, the power of sin was destroyed, and mankind was reconciled to God. First Corinthians 15:21-22 explains, "Since death came through a man, the resurrection of the dead comes also through a man. For as in Adam all die, so in Christ will all be made alive."

❧ The Cabby would be content to live in Narnia forever—if his wife is by his side. So Aslan brings her to him. In the Garden of Eden, Adam needed a wife; so God created one and brought her to him (Genesis 2:20b-23).

⌘ Aslan appoints the first King and Queen of Narnia. He gives them the task of naming and ruling over the animals, working the soil, and populating the earth. Genesis 2:15 tells us, "The LORD God took the man and put him in the Garden of Eden to work it and take care of it." He gave Adam the task of naming all the animals (Genesis 2:19-20). "God blessed them [Adam and Eve] and said to them, 'Be fruitful and increase in number; fill the earth and subdue it. Rule over the fish of the sea and the birds of the air and over every living creature that moves on the ground'" (Genesis 1:28).

Do You Know?

The Cabby is a kind, decent, hard-working man whose first inclination in time of trouble is to sing a hymn. (See Chapter Eight.) He feels as if he knows Aslan already—as Aslan says he does—perhaps because he knows Aslan by his other name in our world. Do you know what that name is?

(Hint: Read Philippians 2:9-11. For more on C.S. Lewis's identification of Aslan's other name, see the introduction to this book.)

Scriptures on Confession and Repentance

2 Corinthians 7:10   Acts 3:19   1 John 1:9

12. STRAWBERRY'S ADVENTURE

As a father has compassion on his children, so the LORD has compassion on those who fear him; for he knows how we are formed, he remembers that we are dust. PSALM 103:13-14

Biblical Parallels and Principles

Digory discovers that Aslan knows and understands—even shares—his grief. Isaiah 53:3 describes Jesus as "a man of sorrows, and familiar with suffering." The Scripture tells of many occasions when Jesus was moved with compassion for those who were hurting. (For example, see Matthew 9:36; 20:34; 23:37; Mark 1:41; and Luke 7:13.) Jesus visited Mary and Martha, whose brother had just died. John 11:33 tells us, "When Jesus saw her weeping, and the Jews who had come along with her also weeping, he was deeply moved in spirit and troubled." Then verse 35 says, "Jesus wept."

Fledge tells Digory that he has no doubt Aslan knows what they need: "But I've a sort of idea he likes to be asked." In Matthew 6:8 Jesus says, "Your Father knows what you need before you ask him." Then He goes on to give instructions on how to pray. Just because God already knows doesn't mean we shouldn't ask. Psalm 62:8 tells us, "Pour out your hearts to him." James 4:2 explains, "You do not have, because you do not ask God." Matthew 7:7 says, "Ask and it will be given to you; seek and you will find; knock and the door will be opened to you."

Think About It!

Aslan renames Strawberry Fledge and calls him "the father of all flying horses." The Bible tells us that often when people had an encounter with God, He changed their name to reflect their new nature or calling. Can you think of any examples?

    (Hint: Read Genesis 17:5, 15-16, 32:28, and Matthew 16:17-18.)

Scriptures on Wings

Psalm 17:6-8   Psalm 91:1-4   Isaiah 40:29-31

13. AN UNEXPECTED MEETING

"I tell you the truth, the man who does not enter . . . by the gate,
but climbs in by some other way, is a thief and a robber." JOHN 10:1

Biblical Parallels and Principles

❧ Digory enters the garden by the gate; the Witch has climbed over the wall. In John 10 Jesus compared Himself to a shepherd who cares for his sheep. He also said, "I am the gate for the sheep . . . whoever enters through me will be saved. . . . The thief comes only to steal and kill and destroy; I have come that they may have life, and have it to the full" (vv. 7-10). Further on, in John 14:6, He again explains, "I am the way and the truth and the life. No one comes to the Father except through me."

❧ Digory's encounter with the Witch in Aslan's garden is very similar to Eve's encounter with the serpent in the Garden of Eden. Digory, like Eve, is most tempted when he stops to look at the fruit, smell it, and contemplate what it might do for him (see Genesis 3:6). In the same way that Jadis questions Digory, the serpent questions Eve—whether it really would be wrong to eat the forbidden fruit. The serpent promises Eve that eating the fruit will give her knowledge and life and power. He suggests that God has lied to her, that God is cruelly keeping her from something wonderful that she wants and needs. "For God knows that when you eat of it your eyes will be opened, and you will be like God, knowing good and evil" (Genesis 3:5).

❧ Both Eve and Jadis learn the truth of Proverbs 9:17: "Stolen water is sweet; food eaten in secret is delicious. But little do they know" that it has a bitter aftertaste. "There is a way that seems right to a man, but in the end it leads to death" (Proverbs 14:12).

❧ Jadis tempts Digory to do the wrong thing (steal) for the right motive (saving his mother). Satan tempted Jesus that way in the wilderness (see Matthew 4:1-11). But rebellion and disobedience is never the right choice. Instead, James 4:7 urges, "Submit yourselves, then, to God. Resist the devil, and he will flee from you."

❧ As hard as it is, Digory resists the temptation to steal the fruit. For all he knows, he is giving up his only chance to save his mother. Although obedience may seem costly, it brings a reward far greater than we can imagine. In Matthew 16:25 Jesus explained, "Whoever wants to save his life will lose it, but whoever loses his life for me will find it." Proverbs 3:5-6 encourages us, "Trust in the LORD with all your heart and lean not on your own understanding; in all your ways acknowledge him, and he will make your paths straight."

Sound Familiar?

The tree in Aslan's garden has life-giving power. The Bible tells us that Heaven will be full of such trees. "Their fruit will serve for food and their leaves for healing" (Ezekiel 47:12). There is also a very special Tree of Life (Genesis 2:9; Revelation 22:14). Do you know who will enjoy its fruit, and who will not?

(Hint: Read Revelation 22:1-4, 14-15.)

Scriptures on Eternal Life

John 3:16   1 John 5:11-12, 20   1 Timothy 1:15-17

14. THE PLANTING OF THE TREE

*And what does the LORD require of you? To act justly and to love
mercy and to walk humbly with your God.* MICAH 6:8

Biblical Parallels and Principles

⁓ When Digory returns, Aslan greets him with "Well done." In the Parable
of the Talents, Jesus described how God will respond to the obedience
of those who serve Him: "Well done, good and faithful servant! You have
been faithful with a few things; I will put you in charge of many things.
Come and share your Master's happiness!" (Matthew 25:21).

⁓ The children notice that Frank and Helen look very different from "their
old selves." Now in Narnia, they have taken off the "old self with its practices and have put on the new self, which is being renewed in knowledge
in the image of its Creator" (Colossians 3:9-10; see also Ephesians 4:22-
24). Second Corinthians 5:17 says, "If anyone is in Christ, he is a new creation; the old has gone, the new has come!"

⁓ Aslan says he cannot do anything for Uncle Andrew because "he has made
himself unable to hear my voice." Regardless of all that Jesus said and did,
and in spite of the signs and wonders He performed, many people would
not believe in Him. "Though seeing, they do not see; though hearing,
they do not hear or understand" (Matthew 13:13). "Their minds [are]
closed so they cannot understand" (Isaiah 44:18). In some places, we're
told, Jesus could not do many miracles "because of their unbelief"
(Matthew 13:58, ESV; see also Mark 6:5).

⁓ The smell of the Tree is "joy and life and health" to the Narnians, but
"death and horror and despair" to the Witch. The Bible tells us that as
believers, we have the same effect on people. "For we are to God the
aroma of Christ among those who are being saved and those who are perishing. To the one we are the smell of death; to the other, the fragrance
of life" (2 Corinthians 2:15-16). In other words, fellow believers and
those who want to be saved will be drawn to us. Those who don't want
to be saved will hate even the "smell" of us, as it reminds them of their
wickedness and the eternal punishment that awaits them.

⁓ Digory realizes that there are things "more terrible even than losing
someone you love by death." In his adult life, C.S. Lewis drew comfort from this truth as he reflected on the loss of his own mother. (She
died of cancer when he was just nine years old.) For believers, death is

only the doorway to Heaven. "No eye has seen, no ear has heard, no mind has conceived what God has prepared for those who love him" (1 Corinthians 2:9).

🔥 Aslan rewards Digory's obedience by giving him the fruit he was so tempted to steal—the apple that will bring healing to his mother. Psalm 37:4-5 tells us, "Commit your way to the LORD; trust in him. . . . Delight yourself in the LORD, and he will give you the desires of your heart."

Sound Familiar?

Aslan recognizes what Digory has been through—the struggle and sacrifice that obedience required. "For this fruit you have hungered and thirsted and wept." Digory's story will be told in Narnia for generations to come. The Bible tells us that a woman once did something very special for Jesus, and He said she would always be remembered for it. Do you know what it was?

(Hint: Read Mark 14:3-9.)

Scriptures on the Rewards of Obedience

James 1:12   John 14:21   Psalm 1

15. THE END OF THIS STORY AND THE BEGINNING OF ALL THE OTHERS

Gladness and joy will overtake them, and sorrow and sighing will flee away. ISAIAH 35:10

Biblical Parallels and Principles

Aslan warns the children that our world is on the way to becoming like Charn. The Scriptures tell us, "There will be terrible times in the last days. People will be lovers of themselves, lovers of money, boastful, proud, abusive, disobedient to their parents, ungrateful, unholy, without love, unforgiving, slanderous, without self-control, brutal, not lovers of the good, treacherous, rash, conceited, lovers of pleasure rather than lovers of God—having a form of godliness but denying its power" (2 Timothy 3:1-5a). Our world will eventually be destroyed. But in Revelation 21:1-4 and 22:1-5, we learn that God will create a glorious new Heaven and new earth for all who have remained faithful to Him.

As mentioned in the notes on Chapter Five, readers in C.S. Lewis's day saw an immediate connection between "the deplorable word" and the newly developed atom bomb. But Lewis was not warning that nuclear war was the ultimate threat to modern civilization. In fact, he predicted that biological warfare might one day supersede it. Lewis said, "As a Christian, I take it for granted that human history will some day end" (*God in the Dock*, 1958). The point is not to be concerned about a specific weapon that may be developed, but to realize the capacity for evil that exists in our fallen nature. The ultimate threat—whatever it is—will be born out of the depravity of the human heart.

Digory is thrilled to witness his mother's miraculous recovery. His sacrificial obedience has truly been rewarded. Psalm 34:4-5, 8 says, "I sought the LORD, and he answered me; he delivered me from all my fears. Those who look to him are radiant; their faces are never covered with shame. . . . Taste and see that the LORD is good; blessed is the man who takes refuge in him."

Throughout their adventures, Polly and Digory have shared the blessing of true friendship. They have experienced the truth of Ecclesiastes 4:9-11: "Two are better than one. . . . If one falls down, his friend can help him up. . . . Also if two lie down together, they will keep warm. But how can one keep warm alone? Though one may be overpowered, two can defend themselves." As Proverbs 17:17 observes, "A friend loves at all times, and a brother is born for adversity."

Sound Familiar?

Here we learn the origin of the mysterious wardrobe that transported the Pevensie children to their adventures in Narnia in *The Lion, the Witch and the Wardrobe*. When C.S. Lewis was a little boy, he and his brother Warnie would climb up into a big, old wardrobe and tell each other their own adventure stories. More than forty years later, Lewis began writing for children, "stories within stories" that had very special meaning to those who understood them. Someone in the Bible told stories that had secret meanings. Do you know who?

(Hint: Read Mark 4:33-34 and Matthew 13:34-35.)

Scriptures on Beginnings and Endings

Isaiah 43:18-19a   Ecclesiastes 3:11   Revelation 22:13

THE LION,
THE WITCH
AND THE
WARDROBE

Introduction to

The Lion, the Witch and the Wardrobe

In reality however he [Aslan] is an invention giving an imaginary answer to the question, "What might Christ become like, if there really were a world like Narnia and He chose to be incarnate and die and rise again in that world as He has actually done in ours?" C. S. LEWIS, IN A LETTER TO A FRIEND

This is the premise of the very first book about Narnia—the most famous and beloved book in *The Chronicles*—the one that started it all: *The Lion, the Witch and the Wardrobe.* (It became known as Book Two when *The Magician's Nephew* was released, and publishers decided to renumber the series according to the chronology of the stories themselves.)

The adventure begins when Peter, Susan, Edmund, and Lucy tumble through the door of a mysterious wardrobe into Narnia—an enchanted world of talking beasts, fauns, dwarfs, giants, and other wonderful creatures. The children discover that Narnia is in bondage—held captive for a hundred years under the spell of the evil White Witch. "She'd made it always winter and never Christmas."

Prophecies have foretold the end of the Witch's reign. One day Aslan will return to Narnia. Aslan is the great Lion, the King of Beasts, Son of the Emperor-Beyond-the-Sea.

> *"Wrong will be right, when Aslan comes in sight,*
> *At the sound of his roar, sorrows will be no more,*

> *When he bares his teeth, winter meets its death,*
> *And when he shakes his mane, we shall have spring again."*

Furthermore, as the saying goes, two "Sons of Adam" and two "Daughters of Eve" will one day sit on the four thrones at Cair Paravel and will rule as Kings and Queens in Narnia. Could it be that Narnia's deliverance is at hand?

Over the years, millions of readers have thrilled to discover the "story within the story" of *The Lion, the Witch and the Wardrobe*. It's the story of the Gospel—the story of salvation. In a general sense, all of Narnia awaits deliverance from the dominion of the White Witch. The land itself longs to be free from captivity—to return to the peace and joy and beauty of the life it once knew. "The creation waits in eager expectation for the sons of God to be revealed . . . in hope that [it] . . . will be liberated from its bondage to decay and brought into the glorious freedom of the children of God" (Romans 8:19-21).

It is also a story of personal salvation—and the personal sacrifice that makes that salvation possible. Edmund falls under the spell of the White Witch. He succumbs to his own pride, selfishness, greed, and lust. He becomes a traitor. And according to the Deep Magic (or law) on which Narnia was founded, Edmund must pay the penalty with his life. "The wages of sin is death" (Romans 6:23). "Without the shedding of blood, there is no forgiveness of sins" (Hebrews 9:22, ESV).

The only hope for Narnia and for Edmund is Aslan. Only Aslan—the one who created Narnia—can now deliver it from the power of the Witch. "The reason the Son of God appeared was to destroy the devil's work" (1 John 3:8). And it is Aslan who will lay down his own life for Edmund, taking Edmund's punishment and dying in his place. "God demonstrates his own love for us in this: While we were still sinners, Christ died for us" (Romans 5:8). Ultimately, it is in dying a torturous and agonizing death at the hands of the Witch that Aslan sets Narnia and Edmund free. For there is an even "Deeper Magic"—a greater law—at work:

> "When a willing victim who had committed no treachery was killed in a traitor's stead, the Table would crack and Death itself would start working backward."

With Aslan's sacrifice on the Stone Table, the power of sin and death is broken. Aslan's resurrection marks the beginning of the Golden Age of Narnia—a time of unprecedented joy, peace, and prosperity.

The Bible tells us that "Christ redeemed us from the curse of the law" (Galatians 3:13) and that God "has rescued us from the dominion of darkness and brought us into the kingdom of the Son he loves, in whom we have redemption, the forgiveness of sins" (Colossians 1:13-14).

In addition to the themes of salvation, redemption, and restoration and/or reconciliation, *The Lion, the Witch and the Wardrobe* also includes illustrations of the following:

෴ The wickedness and deceitfulness of the enemy of our souls (John 8:44).

෴ The power of sin—and its consequences (James 1:14-15).

෴ Maintaining a holy fear of and reverence for God, who is both good and terrible at the same time (Deuteronomy 7:21; Psalm 99:3).

These are just a few of the spiritual treasures you will discover as you begin your own adventure with *The Lion, the Witch and the Wardrobe*!

1. LUCY LOOKS INTO A WARDROBE

Be happy . . . while you are young. . . . Follow the ways of your heart and whatever your eyes see. ECCLESIASTES 11:9

Biblical Parallels and Principles

❧ Lucy discovers that there is much more to the mysterious wardrobe than meets the eye. Jesus told His disciples not to judge things by their appearance (John 7:24). The Bible frequently refers to the discovery of hidden truths and treasures—the revelation of mysteries: "The secret things belong to the LORD our God" (Deuteronomy 29:29). "He reveals deep and hidden things" (Daniel 2:22). "It is the glory of God to conceal a matter; to search out a matter is the glory of kings" (Proverbs 25:2).

❧ Twice Lewis mentions that Lucy has left the door open "because she knew that it is a very foolish thing to shut oneself into any wardrobe." The Scriptures often remind us of the value of wisdom and caution: "A prudent man gives thought to his steps" (Proverbs 14:15b; see also Proverbs 14:8, 16).

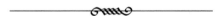

Do You Know?

Lucy is drawn further and further into the wardrobe by the light from the lamp-post. What does the Scripture call a "lamp"? And who is the "light"?

(Hint: Read Psalm 119:105 and John 8:12.)

Scriptures on Searching Out the Secret Things of God

1 Corinthians 2:7-13   Romans 11:33-36   Colossians 2:2-3

2. WHAT LUCY FOUND THERE

With his mouth each speaks cordially to his neighbor, but in his heart he sets a trap for him. JEREMIAH 9:8B

Biblical Parallels and Principles

When Lucy agrees to have tea with Tumnus, she walks right into a trap. The psalmist often prayed for protection from his enemies: "Keep me from the snares they have laid for me" (Psalm 141:9; see also Psalm 59:1-4; 119:86; 143:9). He asked God to expose their evil schemes and drew comfort from the assurance that "the LORD watches over all who love him" (Psalm 145:20; see also Psalm 34:17; 40:1-2; 121).

Tumnus suddenly feels the weight of the sin he is committing. "My guilt has overwhelmed me like a burden too heavy to bear" (Psalm 38:4). In spite of his initial response, Tumnus realizes that it is not too late—he can still do what is right. Second Corinthians 7:10 tells us, "Godly sorrow brings repentance that leads to salvation and leaves no regret." Acts 3:19 urges, "Repent, then, and turn to God, so that your sins may be wiped out, that times of refreshing may come from the Lord."

Did You Notice?

Mr. Tumnus refers to Lucy as a "Daughter of Eve." According to the Bible, all human beings are physically descended from Adam and Eve. (Genesis 3:20 tells us that Eve is "the mother of all the living.") We are also *spiritually* descended from Adam and Eve, in that every one of us suffers under the curse of Eden (Genesis 3:14-19). We have inherited from our first parents a sinful nature, and now, like them, we are in need of a Savior (Romans 5:12-19).

Scriptures on True Repentance

Joel 2:12-13   Psalm 51   1 John 1:9

3. EDMUND AND THE WARDROBE

A man who lacks judgment derides his neighbor, but a man of
understanding holds his tongue. PROVERBS 11:12

Biblical Parallels and Principles

As a brother, Edmund proves to be mean-spirited, selfish, and unkind. He delights in mocking Lucy and looks for ways to provoke her. Proverbs 17:19 says, "He who loves a quarrel loves sin." Proverbs 18:21 cautions, "The tongue has the power of life and death, and those who love it will eat its fruit." Colossians 3:12 tells us how we should behave: "Clothe yourselves with compassion, kindness, humility, gentleness and patience." First Thessalonians 5:15 says, "Always try to be kind to each other."

In many fairy tales a white witch is a good witch, and white magic is good magic—as opposed to "evil," "dark," or "black" magic. But in *The Lion, the Witch and the Wardrobe*, C.S. Lewis uses white to represent winter and death. This paints a picture of a world that is cold and colorless. For in Narnia—and in the Scriptures—there's no such thing as a "good witch." Deuteronomy 18:10-12 warns, "Let no one be found among you who . . . practices divination or sorcery, interprets omens, engages in witchcraft, or casts spells, or who is a medium or spiritist or who consults the dead. Anyone who does these things is detestable to the LORD."

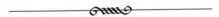

Do You Know?

Lucy is telling the truth, but Edmund doesn't believe her story about the wardrobe. The Bible tells us about Someone whose brothers and sisters didn't believe what He said either. Do you know who?

(Hint: Read John 7:3-5.)

Scriptures on Brotherly Love

John 13:34-35   1 Peter 3:8   1 Corinthians 13

4. TURKISH DELIGHT

Stolen water is sweet; food eaten in secret is delicious.

PROVERBS 9:17

Biblical Parallels and Principles

The White Witch suddenly changes her tone with Edmund and represents herself as a friend. But 1 John 3:7 says, "Dear children, do not let anyone lead you astray." Second Corinthians 11:14-15 explains, "Satan himself masquerades as an angel of light . . . his servants masquerade as servants of righteousness." And "by appealing to the lustful desires of sinful human nature, they entice people" (2 Peter 2:18). "By smooth talk and flattery they deceive the minds of naive people" (Romans 16:18b).

Edmund's greed gets the better of his judgment. Proverbs 23:1-3 cautions, "When you sit to dine with a ruler, note well what is before you, and put a knife to your throat if you are given to gluttony. Do not crave his delicacies, for that food is deceptive."

Think About It!

The Bible tells us repeatedly to resist temptation and instead obey God's commandments. One of the problems with sin is that—like the enchanted Turkish Delight—it's addictive. And it separates us from God. James 1:14-15 explains, "Each one is tempted when, by his own evil desire, he is dragged away and enticed. Then, after desire has conceived, it gives birth to sin; and sin, when it is full-grown, gives birth to death." How does the Bible say we should handle temptation?

(Hint: Read James 4:7.)

Scriptures on Pure Delight

Isaiah 61:10   Psalm 37:4   Zephaniah 3:17

5. BACK ON THIS SIDE OF THE DOOR

Reckless words pierce like a sword, but the tongue of the wise brings healing. PROVERBS 12:18

Biblical Parallels and Principles

❧ Edmund continues being mean and nasty to Lucy. Proverbs 11:17 warns, "A kind man benefits himself, but a cruel man brings trouble on himself."

❧ Lucy refuses to change her story—she knows the truth for herself, even if no one else believes her. To those who suffer persecution and experience the temptation to take the easy way out, the Scriptures say, "Stand firm. Let nothing move you" (1 Corinthians 15:58). "Speak the truth to each other" (Zechariah 8:16), "holding on to faith and a good conscience" (1 Timothy 1:19).

❧ Just as Peter and Susan were concerned about Lucy, the Bible tells us that Jesus' brothers and sisters were concerned about Him. They did not believe what He said about being the Son of God: "When his family heard about this, they went to take charge of him, for they said, 'He is out of his mind'" (Mark 3:21).

Do You Know?

Sometimes our friends and family forsake us (see Job 19:19). Edmund denied having ever been in Narnia with Lucy. When the going got tough, one of Jesus' closest disciples denied even knowing Him. Do you remember who?

(Hint: Read Luke 22:54-62.)

Scriptures on Beastly Behavior

Psalm 57:4   James 4:1-3   Galatians 5:13-15

6. INTO THE FOREST

The path of the righteous is like the first gleam of dawn, shining ever brighter till the full light of day. PROVERBS 4:18

Biblical Parallels and Principles

Though Edmund still refuses to acknowledge any wrongdoing, Peter is quick to apologize for not believing Lucy. "He who conceals his sins does not prosper, but whoever confesses and renounces them finds mercy" (Proverbs 28:13).

The children realize that they have a responsibility to Mr. Tumnus. He has shown compassion to Lucy. Isaiah 16:3 commands us, "Hide the fugitives, do not betray the refugees." Isaiah 1:17 says, "Seek justice, encourage the oppressed." Hebrews 13:3 urges, "Remember those in prison as if you were their fellow prisoners, and those who are mistreated as if you yourselves were suffering." Proverbs 24:11 tells us, "Rescue those being led away to death."

Peter and Edmund debate about whether or not they can trust Tumnus and the Robin—though Edmund has already made a secret and dangerous alliance with the White Witch. Proverbs 12:26 says, "A righteous man is cautious in friendship, but the way of the wicked leads them astray."

Think About It!

Instead of admitting his own guilt, Edmund blames his brother and sisters for being unkind to him. He comforts himself with thoughts of revenge. How does the Bible say we should respond to those who mistreat us?

(Hint: Read Matthew 5:38-44.)

Scriptures on Forgiveness and Reconciliation

Ephesians 4:32   Luke 17:3-4   Colossians 3:12-14

7. A DAY WITH THE BEAVERS

We wait for you; your name and renown are the desire of our hearts. ISAIAH 26:8

Biblical Parallels and Principles

✥ "Aslan is on the move!" At the mention of his name, the children have what theologians call a *numinous*—a mysterious, supernatural—experience of the divine presence. It awakens one's spiritual understanding and elicits a profound personal response. To the righteous, the name of the Lord is "glorious and awesome" (Deuteronomy 28:58), "majestic" (Psalm 8:1), and worthy of praise (Psalm 113:3). To the wicked it speaks of judgment (Isaiah 64:2) and is the object of blasphemy and scorn (Psalm 139:20; Isaiah 52:5).

✥ Further on, in Chapter Eight, the children learn that their arrival in Narnia is seen as the fulfillment of prophecy—a sign that Narnia's long-awaited deliverance is near. "The creation waits in eager expectation for the sons of God to be revealed" (Romans 8:19). This is why upon meeting them, Mrs. Beaver exclaims, "To think that ever I should live to see this day!" In Luke 2:29-30, Simeon rejoiced to witness the arrival of the Christ-child, Israel's Deliverer: "Sovereign Lord, as you have promised, you now dismiss your servant in peace. For my eyes have seen your salvation."

Did You Know?

In a letter to a friend, C.S. Lewis declared that Aslan was *not* an allegorical figure, like those of John Bunyan's *Pilgrim's Progress*, because Lewis held to a strict literary/academic definition of the word *allegory*. Instead, he explained, Aslan "is an invention giving an imaginary answer to the question, 'What might Christ become like, if there really were a world like Narnia and He chose to be incarnate and die and rise again in that world as He has actually done in ours?"

Scriptures on the Power of Jesus' Name

Acts 3:6, 16   John 18:4-6   Philippians 2:9-11

8. WHAT HAPPENED AFTER DINNER

Do you not know? Have you not heard? The LORD is the everlasting God, the Creator of the ends of the earth. ISAIAH 40:28

Biblical Parallels and Principles

Aslan has many names: King, Lord, Son of the Great Emperor-Beyond-the-Sea, King of Beasts, the great Lion. The Bible tells us that—among other things—Jesus is the King of kings and Lord of lords (Revelation 19:16), the Son of God, the Son of Man (Luke 22:69-70), and the Lion of Judah (Revelation 5:5).

Like the prophecies about Aslan, there are countless prophecies in the Bible about the coming of the Messiah, "the anointed one," the Deliverer. Among them: He would set wrong to right (Isaiah 61:1-2). He would "roar like a lion" (Hosea 11:10-11; Jeremiah 25:30). He would end sorrow and suffering (Isaiah 65:19; Revelation 21:4). He would destroy the works of the devil (Psalm 110:1; 1 John 3:8; Psalm 2:7-9). He would bring new life (Haggai 2:6-7; Isaiah 55:12; John 10:10).

Like Aslan, the Lion of Judah is "not a tame lion." He cannot be controlled or manipulated. He doesn't exist to serve us—we exist to serve Him. Romans 11:33-34 exclaims, "Oh, the depth of the riches of the wisdom and knowledge of God! How unsearchable his judgments, and his paths beyond tracing out! Who has known the mind of the Lord? Or who has been his counselor?" His ways are not our ways (Isaiah 55:8-9). We cannot always understand what He chooses to do—or chooses *not* to do. But this we do know: "The LORD is good and his love endures forever; his faithfulness continues through all generations" (Psalm 100:5).

The White Witch has no power over Aslan—she will barely be able to stand in his presence. The Bible tells us that the demons are subject to Christ (Luke 10:17). They fall down before Him (Mark 3:11), trembling (James 2:19). Believers need not fear the evil one, "whom the Lord Jesus will overthrow with the breath of his mouth and destroy by the splendor of his coming" (2 Thessalonians 2:8).

Can That Be Right?

Could the Witch really be a descendant of Adam's "first wife"? Written by a literary scholar, *The Chronicles of Narnia* are not only full of biblical allusions, but also of numerous references to classical literature and ancient mythology. According to a bizarre Jewish myth—concocted many years after the Scriptures were recorded—Adam had an evil and rebellious first wife, a she-demon named Lilith. (In recent years, Lilith has become a symbolic figure for feminists, as well as those for who practice the occult or engage in perversion.) It made for an interesting explanation of the White Witch's origin in a fairy tale, but as C.S. Lewis knew well, the Bible says Adam's first and only wife was Eve (Genesis 3:20).

Scriptures on the Coming of the Messiah

Micah 5:2   Isaiah 9:6-7   Matthew 12:18-21

9. In the Witch's House

Those who live according to the sinful nature have their minds set on what that nature desires. ROMANS 8:5

Biblical Parallels and Principles

Edmund's reaction to the name of Aslan is one of fear and horror. Romans 8:7 says, "The sinful mind is hostile to God." First John 1:5 tells us that "God is light," and as John 3:20 explains, "Everyone who does evil hates the light, and will not come into the light for fear that his deeds will be exposed."

Although deep down he knows better than to trust the White Witch, Edmund cannot resist the lure of Turkish Delight. "A man is a slave to whatever has mastered him" (2 Peter 2:19). Edmund has the opportunity to turn back, but instead he hardens his heart (see Proverbs 28:14) and plunges deeper into sin (Romans 2:5).

The Chief of the Witch's Secret Police refers to Edmund as the "fortunate favorite of the Queen—or else not so fortunate." There is no safety or security for those who make deals with the devil. The Bible tells us he is "a liar and the father of lies" (John 8:44). He promises the world (Matthew 4:8-9), but he devours all who fall into his trap (1 Peter 5:8).

Do You Know?

In the battle of good versus evil, everyone is forced to choose sides and take a stand. Jesus told His disciples that they would face great danger because of Him: "You will be betrayed even by parents, brothers, relatives and friends" (Luke 21:16). One of Jesus' closest disciples became a traitor and betrayed Him to His enemies. Do you know who?

(Hint: Read Luke 22:3-6.)

Scriptures on Escaping from the Devil's Trap

2 Timothy 2:22-26   1 Peter 5:5-9   Galatians 5:16, 19-25

10. THE SPELL BEGINS TO BREAK

*How beautiful on the mountains are the feet of those who bring
good news, who proclaim peace, who bring good tidings, who
proclaim salvation, who say to Zion, "Your God reigns!"* ISAIAH 52:7

Biblical Parallels and Principles

⌘ The others find Mrs. Beaver's careful and methodical preparations exasperating. But Proverbs 14:15 tells us, "A prudent man gives thought to his steps." Proverbs 19:2 advises, "It is not good to have zeal without knowledge, nor to be hasty and miss the way."

⌘ Father Christmas brings each of the children gifts. These gifts are "tools not toys"—tools that will help them fulfill their calling and face the challenges that lie ahead. According to the Scriptures, Jesus sent the Holy Spirit to give believers spiritual gifts for the same purpose. The Spirit gives these gifts "to each one, just as he determines" (1 Corinthians 12:11; compare vv. 4-31). Some are given gifts of leadership; others are given gifts of faith, wisdom, or discernment. Some have "gifts of healing" and the ability to help others (1 Corinthians 12:28). Each believer is a part of "the body of Christ" (1 Corinthians 12:27). And each one has his or her own special gift and calling (1 Corinthians 12:18).

Think About It!

Children often wrote to C.S. Lewis to ask him about Aslan's true identity—his other name in our world. Lewis always answered by giving hints, including this one: "Who in our world arrived at the same time as Father Christmas?"

(Hint: Read Luke 2:1-20.)

Scriptures on the Weapons of Spiritual Warfare

Ephesians 6:10-18   2 Corinthians 10:3-5   Hebrews 4:12

11. ASLAN IS NEARER

See! The winter is past; the rains are over and gone. Flowers appear on the earth; the season of singing has come, the cooing of doves is heard in our land. SONG OF SONGS 2:11-12

Biblical Parallels and Principles

❧ Edmund's eyes are opened, and he begins to see the White Witch for who she really is. Psalm 5:9 says of the wicked, "Not a word from their mouth can be trusted; their heart is filled with destruction. Their throat is an open grave; with their tongue they speak deceit."

❧ The Witch does not have a drop of kindness or compassion in her entire being. She even mistreats the reindeer that pull her sleigh. Proverbs 12:10 observes, "A righteous man cares for the needs of his animal, but the kindest acts of the wicked are cruel."

❧ For the first time Edmund feels pity—or compassion—for someone besides himself. The Scriptures tell us, "Each of you should look not only to your own interests, but also to the interests of others" (Philippians 2:4). "Let us love one another" (1 John 4:7). "Rejoice with those who rejoice; mourn with those who mourn" (Romans 12:15).

Do You Know?

It becomes clear that the enchantment is broken—the Witch's power is crumbling. The Dwarf exclaims, "This is Aslan's doing." The Bible says that Someone came to our world to destroy the works of the devil. Do you know who?

(Hint: Read 1 John 3:8.)

Scriptures on Celebrating God's Deliverance

Psalm 98   Joel 2:21-27   Revelation 15:3-4.

12. PETER'S FIRST BATTLE

So be strong, show yourself a man. 1 KINGS 2:2

Biblical Parallels and Principles

⛤ Compare the description of the creatures gathered around Aslan at the pavilion to these verses: "In that day the Root of Jesse will stand as a banner for the peoples; the nations will rally to him, and his place of rest will be glorious" (Isaiah 11:10). "Your procession has come into view, O God. . . . In front are the singers, after them the musicians; with them are the maidens playing the tambourines" (Psalm 68:24-25). "Let every creature praise his holy name for ever and ever" (Psalm 145:21). Some readers may also be reminded of the scenes in Isaiah, Ezekiel, Daniel, and Revelation that describe the fantastic beings who surround God's heavenly throne. These include seraphim and cherubim and other supernatural creatures that appear like lions, eagles, oxen, and men. (For example, see Isaiah 6:1-3, Ezekiel 1:4-14, and Revelation 4:6-8.)

⛤ Aslan is both "good and terrible at the same time." Years ago the word *terrible* was used to mean "frightening" or "awe-inspiring." The Scriptures tell us that people who had an encounter with the Living God nearly always responded in fear and reverence. (For example, see Hebrews 12:21.) In the King James Version, Deuteronomy 7:21 explains, "The LORD thy God is among you, a mighty God and terrible." And Psalm 99:3 (KJV) says, "Let them praise thy great and terrible name; for it is holy." (Modern Bible translations replace the word "terrible" with "awesome.")

⛤ Aslan calls his servants to take the weary worn-out girls and "minister" to them. After Jesus had endured temptation in the wilderness, God's servants—angels—were called to minister to Him (Matthew 4:11, KJV, ESV).

⛤ Peter faces his first test. Aslan ensures that Peter has the opportunity to begin developing the courage, maturity, and leadership ability that he will need as High King. God does the same for each one of us, preparing us for service in His kingdom. Psalm 18:34-38 says in part, "He trains my hands for battle; my arms can bend a bow of bronze. . . . I pursued my enemies and overtook them . . . they fell beneath my feet."

Do You Know?

Some literary scholars have compared the Stone Table to ancient altars at sites of pagan worship, such as Stonehenge. But in a letter to a girl named Patricia, C.S. Lewis wrote that it was meant to remind readers of the stone table (or tablet) that God gave to Moses. Do you remember what that table (tablet) had written on it?

(Hint: Read Exodus 24:12; Deuteronomy 10:4 and/or Exodus 20:1-17.)

Scriptures on Courage in Battle

Joshua 1:9   Psalm 27:1-3   Isaiah 12:2

13. DEEP MAGIC FROM THE DAWN OF TIME

Against you, you only, have I sinned and done what is evil in your sight, so that you are proved right when you speak and justified when you judge. PSALM 51:4

Biblical Parallels and Principles

Aslan says there is no need to speak of Edmund's earlier behavior. He has been forgiven. Isaiah 43:18 tells us, "Forget the former things; do not dwell on the past." In verse 25 God explains, "I, even I, am he who blots out your transgressions . . . and remembers your sins no more."

During the encounter with the White Witch, Edmund keeps his eyes on Aslan. Psalm 105:4 says, "Look to the LORD and his strength; seek his face always." Psalm 34:5 explains, "Those who look to him are radiant; their faces are never covered with shame."

As a traitor, Edmund stands condemned. "All who sin under the law will be judged by the law" (Romans 2:12). "The wages of sin is death" (Romans 6:23). Hebrews 9:22 explains, "Without the shedding of blood there is no forgiveness of sins" (ESV). "It is the blood that makes atonement" (Leviticus 17:11).

Notice Aslan's response to Susan's suggestion that he work against the Emperor's Magic. In Matthew 5:17-18 Jesus said, "Do not think that I have come to abolish the Law or the Prophets; I have not come to abolish them but to fulfill them. I tell you the truth, until heaven and earth disappear, not the smallest letter, not the least stroke of a pen, will by any means disappear from the Law until everything is accomplished."

The punishment for Edmund's sin cannot be ignored, forgotten, or suspended somehow. The penalty must be paid—and Aslan takes that responsibility upon himself. Isaiah 53:4 says of Jesus, "Surely he took up our infirmities and carried our sorrows." First Peter 2:24 says, "He himself bore our sins."

As "the Emperor's hangman," the Witch cruelly delights in carrying out judgment against those who have sinned. Whether she recognizes it or not, it is still the *Emperor's* judgment she carries out; ultimately it is his purpose she is serving. The Scripture tells us that Satan's authority comes from God, and that his power is limited by God (see Isaiah 54:16-17; Job 1—2; Luke 22:31-

32; 1 John 4:4). Though the devil would love nothing more than to destroy God and His people, he cannot. He is merely a tool that ultimately serves God's purposes.

Think About It!

Though the White Witch calls herself "Queen," she has no right to the title. Soon, Aslan says, all names will be restored to "their proper owners." John 14:30 refers to Satan as "the prince of this world." The devil represents himself as its ruler (Luke 4:5-6). But who is really the Prince?

(Hint: Read Acts 5:30-31 and Isaiah 9:6-7.)

Scriptures on the Law

Psalm 19:7-10   Isaiah 42:21   Matthew 22:35-40

14. THE TRIUMPH OF THE WITCH

Greater love has no one than this, that he lay down his life for his friends. JOHN 15:13

Biblical Parallels and Principles

~ Compare Aslan's sorrow and desire for companionship to Matthew 26:36-38. Jesus took three of His closest disciples with Him as He went to Gethsemane to pray. "He began to be sorrowful and troubled. Then he said to them, 'My soul is overwhelmed with sorrow to the point of death. Stay here and keep watch with me.'"

~ Aslan offers no resistance when attacked by the evil creatures. He says nothing in answer to their taunts. Speaking prophetically of Jesus, Isaiah 53:7 says, "He was oppressed and afflicted, yet he did not open his mouth. He was led like a lamb to the slaughter, and as a sheep before her shearers is silent, so he did not open his mouth." (See also Matthew 26:62-63a; 27:13-14; Luke 23:8-9.)

~ The creatures cruelly abuse Aslan, just as wicked men abused Jesus. "They spit in his face and struck him with their fists. Others slapped him and said, 'Prophesy to us, Christ. Who hit you?'" (Matthew 26:67). They plucked out His beard (Isaiah 50:6-7). The Roman soldiers stripped Him and flogged Him. They made Him wear a scarlet robe and "twisted a crown of thorns and set it on his head" (Matthew 27:29). Then they knelt in front of Him, saying "Hail, king of the Jews!" They spit on Him; they "struck him on the head again and again" (Matthew 27:29-30). Then they led Him away to be crucified.

~ It seems that evil has triumphed and all hope is lost. Certainly Jesus' disciples thought so when He died on the cross. But Jesus, predicting His crucifixion, saw it differently: "The hour has come for the Son of Man to be glorified. . . . Now my heart is troubled, and what shall I say? 'Father, save me from this hour'? No, it was for this very reason I came to this hour" (John 12:23, 27-28).

Sound Familiar?

Susan and Lucy were the only ones to witness Aslan's suffering and sacrifice. When Jesus was crucified, most of His disciples were in hiding, afraid that they might be next. But a faithful group of women kept watch at the foot of the cross. Do you remember who?

(Hint: Read Matthew 27:55-56; Mark 15:40; and John 19:25.)

Scriptures on Christ's Suffering and Sacrifice

Isaiah 53   1 John 4:10   1 Peter 2:21-25

15. DEEPER MAGIC FROM BEFORE THE DAWN OF TIME

There was a violent earthquake, for an angel of the Lord came down from heaven and, going to the tomb, rolled back the stone and sat on it. MATTHEW 28:2

Biblical Parallels and Principles

⭐ The girls tenderly care for Aslan's bruised and broken body. Mice nibble away at the ropes that bound him. Similarly, Jesus' friends showed tender concern for His earthly body. Joseph of Arimathea took His body down from the cross (John 19:38-42). The women went to the tomb at sunrise to anoint His body with spices (Mark 16:1-2).

⭐ Hearing a noise behind them, Susan and Lucy think that someone has disturbed Aslan's body. The Bible tells us that when Mary Magdalene found His tomb empty, she thought someone must have removed Jesus' body. "They have taken my Lord away," she wept. Then a voice behind her spoke. She turned around, and there stood Jesus Himself (John 20:10-16)!

⭐ Susan fears that they are seeing a ghost. Jesus' disciples felt the same way when He first appeared to them after His resurrection (Luke 24:37-39). Jesus reassured them that it really was Him—in a glorified body that still bore the marks of His crucifixion. "Jesus said, 'Peace be with you!' . . . And with that he breathed on them" (John 20:21-22).

⭐ Aslan talks about the Deep Magic and the Emperor's Deeper Magic. Explaining the meaning behind Jesus' death on the cross, the apostle Paul said, "We do, however, speak a message of wisdom among the mature, but not the wisdom of this age or of the rulers of this age, who are coming to nothing. No, we speak of God's secret wisdom, a wisdom that has been hidden and that God destined for our glory before time began. None of the rulers of this age understood it, for if they had, they would not have crucified the Lord of glory" (1 Corinthians 2:6-8).

⭐ The Deeper Magic stated that "when a willing victim who had committed no treachery was killed in a traitor's stead, the Table would crack and Death itself would start working backward." Romans 5:7-8 observes, "Very rarely will anyone die for a righteous man, though for a good man someone might possibly dare to die. But God demonstrates his own love for us in this: While we were still sinners, Christ died for us." He Himself had committed no sin; instead, He bore *our* sins (1 Peter 2:22-24). Galatians 3:13 says, "Christ redeemed us from the curse of the law." According to Isaiah 53:5, He was wounded for our transgressions—He took the punishment for our sin, "and by his wounds we are healed." First Corinthians 15:54 declares, "Death has been swallowed up in victory!"

As Aslan said, "Death itself would start working backward" (compare Acts 2:24). After his resurrection Aslan heads straight for the Witch's castle, where he will set free those she has held captive and turned to stone. The Bible tells us that as Jesus completed His atoning work on the cross, "The tombs broke open and the bodies of many holy people who had died were raised to life" (Matthew 27:52). Also, during the time between His death and resurrection, Jesus descended into Hades and preached to the righteous who were imprisoned there (awaiting His atonement). He set the captives free and led them into Heaven (1 Peter 3:19; Ephesians 4:8-10).

Sound Familiar?

When Aslan willingly laid down his life for Edmund, the Stone Table broke in two. When Jesus willingly laid down His life for us, the spiritual barrier between God and man was destroyed—and a physical symbol of that barrier was torn in two. Do you remember what that symbol was?

(Hint: Read Matthew 27:51.)

Scriptures on the Atoning Work of Christ

John 3:16-17   Romans 3:23-26   Hebrews 9:14

16. WHAT HAPPENED ABOUT THE STATUES

The lion has roared. AMOS 3:8

Biblical Parallels and Principles

❧ Death now starts working backward—Aslan's breath brings the statues to life. When the first human being was created, "The LORD . . . breathed into his nostrils the breath of life" (Genesis 2:7). In Ezekiel 37:5 God speaks to the slain in the Valley of Bones: "I will make breath enter you, and you will come to life." John 20:22 tells us that after His resurrection, Jesus breathed on His disciples. (For more on the new life that resulted from the Resurrection, see Matthew 27:52 and the notes on Chapter Fifteen of this book.)

❧ Alive again, Aslan begins to go about setting "wrongs to right" (see Chapter Eight). When Jesus began His earthly ministry, He quoted Isaiah 61:1-2 (a prophecy concerning Himself and His calling): "The Spirit of the Sovereign LORD is on me, because the LORD has anointed me to preach good news to the poor. He has sent me to bind up the brokenhearted, to proclaim freedom for the captives and release from darkness for the prisoners, to proclaim the year of the LORD's favor and the day of vengeance of our God."

❧ With a mighty roar, Aslan leads the Narnian creatures on to war against the Witch. Isaiah 31:4 says, "As a lion growls, a great lion over his prey . . . so the LORD Almighty will come down to do battle." "Like a warrior he will stir up his zeal; with a shout he will raise the battle cry and will triumph over his enemies" (Isaiah 42:13).

❧ The Lion has triumphed (Revelation 5:5). The White Witch is defeated. "You said, 'I will continue forever—the eternal queen!' But you did not consider these things or reflect on what might happen" (Isaiah 47:7). "Rejoice over her, O heaven! Rejoice, saints and apostles and prophets! God has judged her for the way she treated you" (Revelation 18:20).

Do You Know?

The Narnian creatures must fight a vast, supernaturally evil army. The Bible tells us that as believers, we are all engaged in an ongoing battle. Who or what is the enemy?

(Hint: Read Ephesians 6:11-12.)

Scriptures on Joy

Psalm 16:11   Psalm 66:1-4   Psalm 126:1-3

17. THE HUNTING OF THE WHITE STAG

Blessed is the man who perseveres under trial, because when he has stood the test, he will receive the crown of life that God has promised to those who love him. JAMES 1:12

Biblical Parallels and Principles

꙳ Unlike Judas in the Bible, Edmund has repented of his sin. He is forgiven and restored to a right relationship with Aslan and his own brothers and sisters. In fact, as Lucy observes, he has become a changed person. In Ezekiel 36:26 God says, "I will give you a new heart and put a new spirit in you; I will remove from you your heart of stone and give you a heart of flesh."

꙳ Lucy's trust in and obedience to Aslan is tested when he asks her to leave Edmund's side and care for others. Sometimes God asks us to do things we don't want to do. In John 14:15 Jesus said, "If you love me, you will obey what I command." He promises that those who trust in Him will never be put to shame (Romans 10:11).

꙳ On a grassy hillside, Aslan miraculously provides food for the entire company. The Bible tells us that Jesus miraculously fed more than five thousand people on a grassy hillside with five loaves of bread and two small fish. (See Matthew 14:15-21, Mark 6:35-44, Luke 9:12-17, or John 6:1-14.)

꙳ Aslan comes and goes—suddenly and mysteriously—just as Jesus did after His resurrection (for various instances, see Matthew 28:9; Mark 16:9-14; Luke 24:15, 36; John 20:14, 19, 26; 21:1, 4). Mr. Beaver explains that Aslan has "other countries to attend to." Jesus compared Himself to a shepherd and told His disciples, "I have other sheep that are not of this sheep pen. I must bring them also. They too will listen to my voice, and there shall be one flock and one shepherd" (John 10:16).

Do You Know?

Though Edmund was a traitor, Aslan suffered and died to save him from the power of the White Witch. Lucy asks Susan, "Does he know what Aslan did for him?" Do *you* know what Jesus did for *you*?

(Hint: Read Romans 5:8; 1 John 2:2; and Isaiah 53:4-5.)

Scriptures on the Glory That Awaits Us

1 Peter 2:9   2 Corinthians 3:18   Revelation 22:1-5

THE
HORSE
AND HIS BOY

Introduction to

The Horse and His Boy

*T*he Horse and His Boy is the third book in *The Chronicles of Narnia*. The story takes place during the "Golden Age" of Narnia—when Peter and Susan and Lucy and Edmund reign from the four thrones at Cair Paravel.

> In those days, far south in Calormen on a little creek of the sea, there lived a poor fisherman called Arsheesh, and with him there lived a boy who called him Father.

Many spiritual treasures—insights and life lessons—can be found in *The Horse and His Boy*. But there is one powerful, overriding theme throughout the story, that of divine providence: God at work behind the scenes.

Shasta is a peasant boy living in a pagan land. When he discovers that he is not really Arsheesh's son, and that the fisherman intends to sell him as a slave, Shasta embarks on an incredible journey to freedom and the discovery of his true identity. His travels lead him to the land of his birth, where in a miraculous chain of events he saves the entire nation from total destruction. He then takes his place as heir to the throne of his father's kingdom.

For most of his life (and his journey) Shasta is unaware that he is being guided and protected. There is Someone watching over him. Only near the very end of his adventure does he come to realize that Aslan has been leading him every step of the way. As Shasta later remarks, "He seems to be at the back of all the stories."

In many ways *The Horse and His Boy* is very similar to the book of Esther.

In the biblical story, an orphaned Jewish girl is chosen to reign as Queen over the pagan land of Persia. Through incredible circumstances she saves the entire Jewish race from total annihilation. Although God's name is never mentioned in the book of Esther, it becomes clear that He is the author and orchestrator of every miraculous circumstance. Both Shasta and Esther experience dark moments when they feel abandoned or when it seems their lives are spiraling out of control. But in the end both experience the truth of Romans 8:28: "And we know that in all things God works for the good of those who love him, who have been called according to his purpose."

Another major theme of *The Horse and His Boy* can be found in the stark contrast between the countries of Calormen and Narnia. Calormen is a country lost in darkness. Its citizens are held captive by ignorance, religious superstition, and fear. They live in a culture of slavery, both physical and spiritual. The masses struggle with an overwhelming sense of hopelessness; the elite are obsessed with greed, lust, and the pursuit of power. Calormen represents a fallen world, a world without God.

Narnia, on the other hand, is a kingdom of light. Its citizens exult in their freedom. They are motivated by a sense of right and wrong and a respect for others. They prize personal honor and integrity. In Narnia, mercy and justice meet. It is a nation under God.

So when Shasta and Aravis make their escape from Calormen to Narnia, in a very real sense they are moving from darkness to light, from death to life. "If any man be in Christ, he is a new creature: old things are passed away; behold, all things are become new" (2 Corinthians 5:17, KJV)

The story of their adventures also includes powerful illustrations of the following truths: "A man reaps what he sows" (Galatians 6:7); and "Pride goes before . . . a fall" (Proverbs 16:18).

These lessons are just a few of the spiritual treasures you will discover as you begin your own wonderful journey with *The Horse and His Boy*.

1. HOW SHASTA SET OUT
ON HIS TRAVELS

*Stand at the crossroads and look; ask for the ancient paths, ask
where the good way is, and walk in it, and you will find rest for
your souls.* JEREMIAH 6:16

Biblical Parallels and Principles

Shasta's deep and inexplicable longing for the North is a desire for something he has never experienced and can't really describe or comprehend. But it's a lot like the spiritual emptiness and longing experienced by every human being. According to the Scriptures, "[God] has set eternity in the hearts of men" (Ecclesiastes 3:11). Many people are searching for something they don't quite understand, looking for something that will fill the emptiness within. The apostle Paul explains, "God did this so that men would seek him and perhaps reach out for him and find him, though he is not far from each one of us" (Acts 17:27).

When Bree invites Shasta to join him on his journey, he echoes the words of wisdom found in Ecclesiastes 4:9-12: "Two are better than one. . . . If one falls down, his friend can help him up. But pity the man who falls and has no one to help him up! Also, if two lie down together, they will keep warm. But how can one keep warm alone? Though one may be overpowered, two can defend themselves."

Can That Be Right?
Arsheesh rebukes Shasta for asking questions about the North. He quotes a proverb that says, in effect, "Pay attention to your work, and don't bother about anything else. It's none of your business." Do you remember what Jesus said about asking questions and searching for truth?

(Hint: Read Matthew 7:7-8.)

Scriptures on Seeking and Finding God
Psalm 63:1   Deuteronomy 4:29   Isaiah 55:6-7

2. A WAYSIDE ADVENTURE

Let us examine our ways and test them, and let us return to the LORD. LAMENTATIONS 3:40

Biblical Parallels and Principles

Now that he is on his way home, the horse Bree worries that he may have acquired "a lot of low, bad habits" while living in Calormen. Repeatedly in the Scriptures, God warns His people not to adopt the customs and habits of godless nations. "'Come out from them and be separate, says the Lord'" (2 Corinthians 6:17). To new Christians who have grown up in a corrupt culture, Colossians 3:7-8a says, "You used to walk in these ways, in the life you once lived. But now you must rid yourselves of all such things. . . ."

Bree refers several times to the "dumb horses" of Calormen. He uses the word primarily to mean "silent," as in "unable to talk." But the word also implies ignorance. These horses do not think or reason. They do not act freely, of their own accord. Instead, they blindly follow where others lead. To Bree, their behavior is truly dumb—as in "foolish"! Psalm 32:9 says, "Do not be like the horse or the mule, which have no understanding, but must be controlled by bit and bridle." Instead, the Scripture says, God's people should learn from the wisdom and instruction He gives.

Think About It!

At first Shasta and Aravis regard each other with suspicion and hostility. They have grown up in a country that follows a strict caste system: A person's value is determined by his or her birth and station in life. But things are very different in Narnia—and in the kingdom of God. The apostle Paul said there is no room for prejudice or discrimination among believers. Do you know why?

(Hint: Read Galatians 3:26-28.)

Scriptures on Renewing the Mind

Colossians 2:6-8   Romans 12:2   Philippians 2:5-11

3. AT THE GATES OF TASHBAAN

The man who thinks he knows something does not yet know as he ought to know. 1 CORINTHIANS 8:2

Biblical Parallels and Principles

❧ Aravis describes her daring escape from an arranged marriage in a very matter-of-fact way. It doesn't occur to her to think of her behavior in terms of right or wrong. She shows no concern for how her actions may affect others—or what consequences might result. She will soon learn the truth of Proverbs 21:2: "All a man's ways seem right to him, but the LORD weighs the heart."

❧ It becomes clear that Bree is quite full of himself—his accomplishments, his experience, his wisdom. Bree's self-focus makes him insensitive to others' feelings, especially Shasta's. Romans 12:3 warns, "Do not think of yourselves more highly than you ought." And 1 Peter 3:8 says, "Live in harmony with one another; be sympathetic, love as brothers, be compassionate and humble."

❧ In his concern over his appearance, Bree loses sight of what is truly important—reaching their destination! It is Hwin who reminds her companions that "the main thing is to get there." In contrast to Bree, Hwin demonstrates "the unfading beauty of a gentle and quiet spirit, which is of great worth in God's sight" (1 Peter 3:4). She consistently models a humble heart. Proverbs 11:2 tells us that "with humility comes wisdom."

❧ As the chapter closes, all four of the travelers have come to realize the truth of Proverbs 13:10: "Pride only breeds quarrels, but wisdom is found in those who take advice."

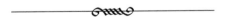

Sound Familiar?

Like Hwin with Aravis, the Bible tells of a time when an animal spoke up and stopped someone from making a terrible mistake. Do you remember the story?

(Hint: Read Numbers 22:21-34.)

Scriptures on Having a Humble Heart

Micah 6:8   Ephesians 4:2   James 3:13

4. SHASTA FALLS IN WITH THE NARNIANS

Those who look to him are radiant. PSALM 34:5

Biblical Parallels and Principles

As the travelers make their way through the capital city, they can feel the despair. The streets are filthy; the air itself is foul and oppressive. Calormen's citizens are held captive by ignorance, religious superstition, and fear. They live in a culture of slavery, both physical and spiritual. The peasants struggle with an overwhelming sense of hopelessness; the nobility are obsessed with greed, lust, and the pursuit of power. Describing such people, Scripture says, "They have neither knowledge nor understanding. They walk about in darkness" (Psalm 82:5, ESV).

In contrast to the miserable and somber residents of Tashbaan, the Narnian lords radiate with joy and laughter. They walk and talk in a free and easy way. Even their clothing is bright and attractive! As Shasta discovers, Narnians are motivated by a sense of right and wrong and a respect for others. They prize personal honor and integrity. Theirs is a kingdom of light—a nation under God. The Bible tells us that "God is light; in him there is no darkness at all" (1 John 1:5). His people are "children of light" (Ephesians 5:8) who "shine like stars in the universe" (Philippians 2:15).

Think About It!

At first Prince Rabadash appeared to be brave, courteous, and kind. But as Queen Susan has discovered, appearances can be deceiving. People may be fooled by the way a person looks on the outside. What does God see?

(Hint: Read 1 Samuel 16:7.)

Scriptures on Walking in the Light

John 8:12   1 Peter 2:9   1 John 1:5-7

5. PRINCE CORIN

The purpose in a man's heart is like deep water, but a man of understanding will draw it out. PROVERBS 20:5, ESV

Biblical Parallels and Principles

As King Edmund discovers Prince Rabadash's treachery, he reveals it to Queen Susan and the other Narnian lords. Together they discuss the situation—each one sharing his or her wisdom, observations, and experience. Proverbs 20:18 cautions, "Make plans by seeking advice; if you wage war, obtain guidance." Proverbs 15:22 explains, "Plans fail for lack of counsel, but with many advisers they succeed."

Tumnus comes up with a clever plan to outwit the Calormenes and escape from Tashbaan without violent conflict. This is an example of the kind of wisdom Jesus referred to in Matthew 10:16. Jesus told His disciples to be on their guard when dealing with evil and immoral people: "Behold, I send you forth as sheep in the midst of wolves: be ye therefore wise as serpents, and harmless as doves" (KJV).

Do You Know?

At the end of *The Lion, the Witch and the Wardrobe*, C.S. Lewis writes that because of her great beauty, many kings asked for Queen Susan's hand in marriage. Here we learn how, on at least one occasion, that leads to disaster. Physical beauty can be a distraction—or even a "curse." What kind of beauty does God value?

(Hint: Read 1 Peter 3:3-5.)

Scriptures on Gaining Wisdom

Psalm 111:10   James 1:5   Proverbs 13:20

6. SHASTA AMONG THE TOMBS

I will lie down and sleep in peace, for you alone, O LORD, make me dwell in safety. PSALM 4:8

Biblical Parallels and Principles

Like Shasta, the psalmist suffered sleepless nights, moments of profound loneliness, and deep despair. He felt abandoned by his friends (Psalm 38:11; 41:9; 55:12-14). He experienced terror as his enemies surrounded him like "jackals" (Psalm 44:19), "snarling . . . dogs" (Psalm 59:6), and "roaring lions" (Psalm 22:13). In utter darkness, the psalmist felt "set apart with the dead, like the slain who lie in the grave" (Psalm 88:3-5). He could feel "the cords of the grave" and "of death" entangling him (Psalm 18:5; 116:3). But time after time he cried out to God and found Him to be a "refuge and strength, a very present help in trouble" (Psalm 46:1, ESV). Over and over, the psalmist rejoiced in God's supernatural deliverance, protection, and guidance. "I sought the LORD, and he answered me; he delivered me from all my fears" (Psalm 34:4).

Shasta drew warmth and comfort from the physical presence of a mysterious cat at his back. In the same way, the psalmist says those who trust in God will feel His presence envelop them: "He will cover you with his feathers, and under his wings you will find refuge; his faithfulness will be your shield. . . . You will not fear the terror of night . . . no harm will befall you" (Psalm 91:4-5, 10).

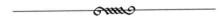

Do You Know?

Anticipating the lion's imminent attack, Shasta exclaims, "I wonder does anything happen to people after they're dead." What does the Bible say about that?

(Hint: Read Hebrews 9:27-28 and John 3:16-18 or Revelation 20:11—22:5.)

Scriptures on Facing Fear

Isaiah 12:2   John 16:33   Psalm 91

7. ARAVIS IN TASHBAAN

Better to be lowly in spirit and among the oppressed than to share plunder with the proud. PROVERBS 16:19

Biblical Parallels and Principles

Lasaraleen shows no real interest in hearing Aravis's story. "She was, in fact, much better at talking than at listening." But James 1:19 tells us, "Everyone should be quick to listen, slow to speak. . . ." Proverbs 10:19 explains, "When words are many, sin is not absent, but he who holds his tongue is wise."

As the wife of a wealthy Tarkaan, Lasaraleen lives a privileged life. She thinks of nothing but "clothes and parties and gossip." She likes drawing attention to herself and showing off. In 1 Timothy 6:17-19, the apostle Paul described how people who have been blessed with abundant resources *should* live: "Command those who are rich in this present world not to be arrogant nor to put their hope in wealth, which is so uncertain, but to put their hope in God, who richly provides us with everything for our enjoyment. Command them to do good, to be rich in good deeds, and to be generous and willing to share. In this way they will lay up treasure for themselves as a firm foundation for the coming age, so that they may take hold of the life that is truly life."

Think About It!

Lasaraleen insists on having the finest clothes. Much to Aravis's dismay, she chatters constantly about which beautiful outfit she wore on this or that occasion. Lasaraleen even makes a great fuss over choosing the perfect dress for Aravis. But is it really all about the clothes? According to the Bible, what are the qualities of an attractive woman?

(Hint: Read Proverbs 31:10-31.)

Scriptures on Treasure That Will Last Forever
2 Corinthians 9:6-11   Luke 18:18-30   Matthew 6:19-21

8. IN THE HOUSE OF THE TISROC

The wicked man craves evil; his neighbor gets no mercy from him.
PROVERBS 21:10

Biblical Parallels and Principles

❧ Rabadash and his father share a hatred for Narnia and a desire to destroy both the country and its people. "Everyone who does evil hates the light" (John 3:20). Their understanding is darkened (Ephesians 4:18). They call "good evil" and "evil good" (Isaiah 5:20). When they observe divine intervention, they either attempt to explain it away with science or attribute it to demons and evil spirits. In 2 Corinthians 4:4, the apostle Paul explained that unbelievers are spiritually blind. They cannot understand the Truth. "The message of the cross is foolishness to those who are perishing, but to us who are being saved, it is the power of God" (1 Corinthians 1:18).

❧ Prince Rabadash, like his name suggests, is both rabid and rash. He sees Queen Susan's rejection of his marriage proposal as an insult to be avenged, and his anger burns out of control. "A quick-tempered man does foolish things," observes Proverbs 14:17. Proverbs 16:18 warns, "Pride goes before destruction, a haughty spirit before a fall."

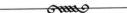

Think About It!
The Bible lists six things that God hates, seven that are detestable to Him. How many of them is Rabadash guilty of?
    (Hint: Read Proverbs 6:16-19.)

Scriptures on Restraint and Self-control
James 1:19-21   Proverbs 17:27   Galatians 5:22-23

9. ACROSS THE DESERT

"The spirit is willing, but the body is weak." MATTHEW 26:41

Biblical Parallels and Principles

In the Scripture, the desert is a place of trial and testing. "God led you all the way in the desert . . . to humble you and to test you in order to know what was in your heart" (Deuteronomy 8:2). As many heroes of the faith have learned firsthand, a journey into the desert is an experience that forms character and develops perseverance. (Think of David, Moses, Elijah, John the Baptist, even Jesus Himself!) God speaks in the solitude. To those who grow weary, Isaiah 35:4, 6-7 says, "'Be strong, do not fear; your God will come . . . he will come to save you.' Water will gush forth in the wilderness and streams in the desert. The burning sand will become a pool."

As the weary travelers discover, there are times when a little rest can be a dangerous thing. They are overcome by sleep—and now may be over-taken by Prince Rabadash. The Bible tells us that as believers, we live in dark and perilous times. We cannot afford to let down our guard and relax. Instead, we must be ready for the challenges that are sure to come our way. First Thessalonians 5:6 urges, "Let us not be like others, who are asleep, but let us be alert and self-controlled."

Do You Know?

Aravis is disgusted that the Tisroc would encourage his son to take action that will likely lead to the Prince's death. But throughout history many kings have done the same. The Bible tells of one who, over time, ordered the execution of his wife, his oldest son, and countless others, including the baby Jesus in a desperate attempt to protect his throne. Do you know who?

(Hint: Read Matthew 2:1-8, 16.)

Scriptures on Desert Testing

Deuteronomy 8:2   Hebrews 11:32-40   Isaiah 40:1-5

10. THE HERMIT OF THE SOUTHERN MARCH

Let us not become weary in doing good, for at the proper time we will reap a harvest if we do not give up. GALATIANS 6:9

Biblical Parallels and Principles

Shasta is discouraged by the increasing difficulty of his experiences. Every task he undertakes is much harder than the previous one. But this is the process that leads to maturity. First Peter 4:12 says, "Dear friends, do not be surprised at the painful trial that you are suffering, as though something strange were happening to you." First Peter 1:6-7 explains, "Now for a little while you may have had to suffer grief in all kinds of trials. These have come so that your faith—of greater worth than gold, which perishes even though refined by fire—may be proved genuine."

Scripture warns that pride goes before a fall (Proverbs 16:18). Bree is bitterly ashamed of himself. But the Hermit urges him not to wallow in self-pity. Instead, he can choose to learn from the experience. "He who listens to a life-giving rebuke will be at home among the wise . . . whoever heeds correction gains understanding" (Proverbs 15:31-32). First Peter 5:6 advises, "Humble yourselves, therefore, under God's mighty hand, that he may lift you up in due time."

Can That Be Right?

Aravis attributes her narrow escape to luck. The Hermit says that in 109 years, he has never met any such thing. Who is right? According to the Bible, who or what controls the circumstances of our lives?

(Hint: Read Psalm 75:6-7 and Proverbs 16:4, 9.)

Scriptures on Perseverance

Hebrews 12:1   James 1:2-4   Philippians 3:13-14

11. THE UNWELCOME FELLOW TRAVELER

"For I know the plans I have for you," declares the LORD,
"plans to prosper you and not to harm you, plans to give you
hope and a future. Then you will call upon me and come and
pray to me, and I will listen to you. You will seek me and find
me when you seek me with all your heart. I will be found by
you . . . and will bring you back from captivity." JEREMIAH 29:11-14

Biblical Parallels and Principles

❧ Shasta's experience with Aslan is very similar to the journey of the two disciples on the road to Emmaus in Luke 24:13-35. The disciples are confused and distressed by Jesus' death on the cross. "As they talked and discussed these things with each other, Jesus himself came up and walked along with them; but they were kept from recognizing him" (v. 15). Jesus listens as they pour out their hearts, and then "beginning with Moses and all the Prophets, he explained what was said in all the Scriptures concerning himself" (v. 27) The discouraged disciples begin to understand that everything that has happened has been a part of God's plan. Their eyes are opened, and they recognize their fellow traveler as the Risen Lord, just before He disappears in glory!

❧ Aslan responds to Shasta's question about Aravis: "Child, I am telling you your story, not hers. I tell no one any story but his own." He says the same thing to Aravis further on in Chapter Fourteen. In John 21:15-23, Jesus tells Peter what will happen to him in the future. Peter's immediate response is to ask what will happen to John. Jesus tells him that what happens to others is not his concern: "You must follow me" (John 21:22).

❧ Aslan gives his name as "Myself." In Exodus 3:13-14 Moses asks God who he should tell the people has sent him. God answers, "I AM WHO I AM. This is what you are to say to the Israelites: 'I AM has sent me to you.'"

Did You Notice?

When Shasta asks Aslan, "Who are you?" Aslan answers the one question three times, each time in a different voice. Most likely, C.S. Lewis is hinting here at the Trinity. The first time Aslan's voice is "deep" and "low" and earthshaking—representing God the Father. The second time the voice is "loud and clear" and joyous, as God the Son. The third time he speaks in a whisper, as God the Holy Spirit.

Scriptures on God at Work Behind the Scenes

Proverbs 20:24   Romans 8:28, 35-39   Psalm 139:1-16

12. SHASTA IN NARNIA

"Be on guard! Be alert! . . . Keep watch." MARK 13:33-35

Biblical Parallels and Principles

🕃 In their prosperity, the woodland creatures have grown complacent and careless—and danger is right at their door! First Peter 5:8 warns, "Be self-controlled and alert. Your enemy the devil prowls around like a roaring lion looking for someone to devour." A believer must always be prepared for battle!

🕃 Though he is a stranger, Shasta receives a warm welcome from the Narnian creatures. They see that he is in need, and they quickly—and cheerfully—come to his assistance. Galatians 6:10 urges, "As we have opportunity, let us do good to all people, especially those who belong to the family of believers."

🕃 Corin loves fun and adventure, but his temper keeps getting him into trouble. Proverbs 20:3 says, "It is to a man's honor to avoid strife, but every fool is quick to quarrel." And Proverbs 19:11 observes, "A man's wisdom gives him patience; it is to his glory to overlook an offense."

Sound Familiar?
As Shasta looks down at the grass, a stream of refreshing water springs forth from Aslan's footprint. Someone in the Bible spoke of Himself as the source of springs of living water. Do you know who?

(Hint: Read John 4:6-14.)

Scriptures on Preparing for Spiritual Warfare
Romans 13:11-12   Ephesians 6:10-18   2 Corinthians 10:3-5

13. THE FIGHT AT ANVARD

"All who rage against you will surely be ashamed and disgraced."
ISAIAH 41:11

Biblical Parallels and Principles

⊰ Marching through the mountain pass, Shasta realizes that once again he has narrowly escaped disaster. One false step the night before, and he would have plunged over the cliff, except for Aslan. "He was between me and the edge all the time." Reflecting on God's miraculous deliverance, the psalmist felt the same relief as Shasta. He exclaimed, "If the LORD had not been on our side . . . !" (Psalm 124:1). Psalm 37:23-24 observes, "If the LORD delights in a man's way, he makes his steps firm; though he stumble, he will not fall, for the LORD upholds him with his hand."

⊰ The Narnian army is made up of many different kinds of creatures, with many different skills and abilities. They use this diversity to their advantage in battle. Each one does what he can do best. This is a perfect example of how believers should work together. According to Scripture, each individual is called and gifted by God; each one has unique strengths and weaknesses. Each one has an important part to play. Together all of the individual parts make up a whole, a unit, a body—the Body of Christ (1 Corinthians 12:4-31).

Sound Familiar?

A freak accident proves to be Rabadash's undoing—a hole in his armor leads to his downfall. The Bible tells of a king who had the same problem. Do you know who?

(Hint: Read 2 Chronicles 18:30-34.)

Scriptures on Divine Protection

Psalm 34:7   Psalm 121   Psalm 23

14. HOW BREE BECAME A WISER HORSE

It was good for me to be afflicted so that I might learn your decrees. PSALM 119:71

Biblical Parallels and Principles

Bree's sudden encounter with Aslan is very similar to the scene described in John 20:24-29. Thomas is refusing to believe that Jesus has literally, physically risen from the dead—the other disciples must have seen a ghost or apparition, a spiritual vision of some kind. Thomas insists he won't believe Jesus is really alive until he has seen "the nail marks in his hands," put his finger where the nails were, and touched His wounded side. Suddenly Jesus appears and calls to Thomas, "Put your finger here; see my hands. Reach out your hand and put it into my side. Stop doubting and believe."

Aravis learns that the injury she received from Aslan was an act of discipline or correction. Colossians 3:25 says, "Anyone who does wrong will be repaid for his wrong." But God's discipline is not a sign of His disfavor. On the contrary, Hebrews 12:6, 10-11 reminds us that "the Lord disciplines those He loves. . . . Our fathers disciplined us for a little while as they thought best; but God disciplines us for our good, that we may share in his holiness. No discipline seems pleasant at the time, but painful. Later on, however, it produces a harvest of righteousness and peace for those who have been trained by it."

Aslan responds to Aravis's question: "Child, I am telling you your story, not hers. No one is told any story but their own." In John 21:15-23 Jesus tells Peter what will happen to him in the future. Peter's immediate response is to ask what will happen to John. Jesus tells him that what happens to others is not his concern: "You must follow me" (John 21:22).

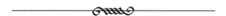

Sound Familiar?

Like Prince Cor, a young man in the Bible was cruelly kidnapped, separated from his family, and sold into slavery in a foreign country. But it turned out that he was in the right place at the right time to save his family and an entire nation from destruction. Do you remember his name?

(Hint: Read Genesis 50:19-20.)

Scriptures on Spiritual Discipline and Correction

Hebrews 12:5-11   Lamentations 3:25-27, 31-33   Psalm 94:12

15. RABADASH THE RIDICULOUS

"God opposes the proud but gives grace to the humble." JAMES 4:6

Biblical Parallels and Principles

⬧ Notice how Rabadash's encounter with Aslan compares to God's conversation with Cain in Genesis 4:6-7. God warns Cain, "Why are you angry? Why is your face downcast? If you do what is right, will you not be accepted? But if you do not do what is right, sin is crouching at your door; it desires to have you, but you must master it."

⬧ Like Cain, Rabadash fails to heed the warning. Rabadash's punishment is very similar to the one God gave to King Nebuchadnezzar in Daniel 4. In the biblical account, the proud and arrogant Babylonian king refuses to acknowledge or give glory to God. As a result, he loses his sanity and becomes like a wild animal, living in the fields outside his palace for seven years. When he finally repents and acknowledges God's sovereignty, his sanity and his kingdom are restored.

Sound Familiar?
Just like Aslan, Someone in the Bible mysteriously appeared and then disappeared in a room full of His friends. Do you know who?

    (Hint: Read John 20:19-20 and Luke 24:36-43.)

Scriptures on Repentance and Forgiveness
1 Peter 5:5-7   2 Chronicles 7:14   1 John 1:9

PRINCE
CASPIAN

Introduction to

Prince Caspian

All the same, I do wish . . . I wish I could have lived in the Old Days . . . when everything was quite different. When the animals could talk, and there were nice people who lived in the streams and the trees. . . . And there were Dwarfs and Fauns.

PRINCE CASPIAN

When *Prince Caspian* begins, a thousand years have passed since King Peter and King Edmund and Queen Susan and Queen Lucy ruled from the four thrones at Cair Paravel. Since then, a wicked race of men has conquered the land, silenced the rivers and trees, and killed off the Talking Beasts and Dwarves and Fauns and Giants. A remnant remain in hiding, holding on to the faintest hope that somehow Narnia will be delivered from the oppression of the Telmarines, set free and restored to its former glory. Some creatures have grown bitter with centuries of suffering. They begin to doubt that Aslan still exists—if he ever did—or that he cares about their plight. Skeptics say the old stories are nothing more than myths or fairy tales. But there are some who still believe, some who insist that the stories are true—that Aslan *will* come again and Narnia will see a new day. "Now faith is being sure of what we hope for and certain of what we do not see" (Hebrews 11:1).

Reading *Prince Caspian*, one can't help but be reminded of the cycle of oppression and deliverance that God's people experienced repeatedly throughout the Old Testament. Or of the four hundred years of silence between the Old Testament and the New Testament—when God said nothing—and yet a faithful remnant clung tightly to the hope of the coming of the Messiah. Then again it's not unlike the period of persecution that followed Jesus' earthly ministry, when the Roman Empire forced the early church underground. In some ways it even seems familiar to us today: The wicked flourish; the righteous are oppressed. Scoffers and skeptics call our faith a fairy tale. Jesus said, "Blessed are those who have not seen and yet have believed" (John 20:29).

Prince Caspian appears on the scene like King Josiah in 2 Chronicles 34. The boy-king of Judah rejected the wickedness and idolatry of his ancestors and single-handedly turned the nation's clock back. While he was still young, Josiah began to seek God. "He did what was right in the eyes of the LORD" (vv. 2-3). He repaired the temple, restored the priesthood, and rediscovered the Book of the Law. "Josiah removed all the detestable idols from all the territory . . . and he had all who were present in Israel serve the LORD their God. As long as he lived, they did not fail to follow the LORD" (v. 33).

But before Caspian can restore Narnia, he must defeat his evil uncle, the usurper, King Miraz. Caspian rallies Old Narnia around him, and they make a valiant effort to take on the Telmarine army. But they are terribly outnumbered. In a desperate moment, Caspian blows the ancient horn of Queen Susan to call for help. The Pevensie children and Aslan will once again appear in Narnia and "put wrongs to right."

For Peter, Edmund, Susan, and Lucy, their second adventure in Narnia is a lesson in courage. "We also rejoice in our sufferings, because we know that suffering produces perseverance; perseverance, character; and character, hope. And hope does not disappoint us" (Romans 5:3-5). Lucy discovers the cost of discipleship (see Matthew 16:24). She and Susan illustrate the story of Mary and Martha in Luke 10:38-42, as Susan allows practical concerns to keep her from experiencing Aslan's presence, while Lucy chooses to "sit at his feet."

Prince Caspian also includes powerful illustrations of the following truths: "Our struggle is not against flesh and blood, but against the rulers, against the authorities, against the powers of this dark world and against the spiritual forces of evil in the heavenly realms" (Ephesians 6:12). "The Lord is not slow in keeping his promise, as some understand slowness. He is patient with you, not wanting anyone to perish, but everyone to come to repentance" (2 Peter 3:9).

These lessons are just a few of the spiritual treasures you will discover as you return to Narnia with *Prince Caspian*.

1. THE ISLAND

Let them give thanks to the Lord for his unfailing love . . . he satisfies the thirsty and fills the hungry with good things.

PSALM 107:8-9

Biblical Parallels and Principles

❧ Susan insists that the others put their shoes back on and wait to eat their sandwiches. Though her siblings find it annoying at times, Susan's attention to practical matters keeps them from making some thoughtless choices or careless mistakes. Proverbs 14:15 tells us, "A prudent man gives thought to his steps."

❧ After walking three-quarters of the way around the island, the children are hot and tired and thirsty. The psalmist compared his spiritual longings to a desperate thirst: "As the deer pants for streams of water, so my soul pants for you, O God. My soul thirsts for God, for the living God" (Psalm 42:1-2). Just as cool water from the stream refreshes the children, the psalmist experienced times of refreshing in the presence of the Lord (Psalm 23:1-3a).

Do You Know?

Though the island is surrounded by water, the children are thirsty—they must find pure, fresh, unsalty water to drink. The book of Exodus tells us that God's people got very thirsty wandering in the desert. How did God provide water for them?

(Hint: Read Exodus 17:1-6.)

Scriptures on Hunger and Thirst

Matthew 5:6   John 4:13-14   Revelation 7:16-17

2. THE ANCIENT TREASURE HOUSE

I will remember the deeds of the Lord; yes, I will remember your miracles of long ago. PSALM 77:11

Biblical Parallels and Principles

※ It's one thing to be cautious—it's another thing to be fearful. As the others grow more and more excited, Susan grows more and more afraid. Her fear is holding her back. Scripture tells us, "Be strong and courageous. Do not be terrified; do not be discouraged, for the LORD your God will be with you wherever you go" (Joshua 1:9).

※ The children recall their days as Kings and Queens of Narnia. Though at first they are saddened that those days are gone, the happy memories remind them of who they are—who they have been and all that they have overcome. It gives them courage to face whatever adventure lies ahead. The psalmist said, "These things I remember as I pour out my soul: how I used to go with the multitude, leading the procession to the house of God, with shouts of joy and thanksgiving among the festive throng. Why are you so downcast, O my soul? . . . Put your hope in God, for I will yet praise him, my Savior and my God" (Psalm 42:4-5).

Think About It!

In the ruins of Cair Paravel, the children have uncovered the ancient treasure chamber where, as Kings and Queens, they kept their most prized possessions. Scripture says that God is a sure foundation for His people, "a rich store of salvation and wisdom and knowledge." What is the key that unlocks this treasure?

(Hint: Read Isaiah 33:5-6.)

Scriptures on Finding Courage in the Face of Fear

Psalm 46:1-3   Isaiah 41:10   Psalm 27:1-6

3. THE DWARF

The righteous man is rescued from trouble, and it comes on the
wicked instead. PROVERBS 11:8

Biblical Parallels and Principles

Susan and the others come to the aid of the Dwarf immediately. Isaiah
1:17 says, "Seek justice, encourage the oppressed." And Proverbs 24:11
says, "Rescue those being led away to death; hold back those staggering
toward slaughter."

All of his life, the Dwarf has been told that the woods on the shore are
haunted. The soldiers flee from the island in fear, convinced they have
been attacked by "ghosts." The Bible speaks scornfully of people who are
"full of superstitions" (Isaiah 2:6) and "terrified by signs in the sky"
(Jeremiah 10:2). Isaiah 8:12-13 tells us, "Do not call conspiracy everything that these people call conspiracy; do not fear what they fear, and do
not dread it. The LORD Almighty is the one you are to regard as holy, he
is the one you are to fear, he is the one you are to dread."

Sound Familiar?

The soldiers are terrified, thinking they've seen a ghost. Even the Dwarf—
who has much more courage and common sense—needs a little reassurance.
The Bible tells us of some people who thought they had seen a ghost. One
of the ways He reassured them that He was real was by eating fish. Do you
know who it was?

(Hint: Read Luke 24:36-45.)

Scriptures on the Terror of the Wicked

Isaiah 3:11   Proverbs 10:24   Proverbs 21:15

4. THE DWARF TELLS OF PRINCE CASPIAN

We did not follow cleverly invented stories when we told you about the power and coming of our Lord Jesus Christ, but we were eyewitnesses of his majesty. 2 PETER 1:16

Biblical Parallels and Principles

The Telmarines have tried to wipe out the memory of Old Narnia and pretend that it never existed. The Bible tells us that godless men "suppress the truth by their wickedness" (Romans 1:18). They have rejected wisdom and reason. "Their thinking became futile and their foolish hearts were darkened. . . . They exchanged the truth of God for a lie" (Romans 1:21, 25). They are no longer capable of understanding what is right and true and real, for their hearts have been hardened (Ephesians 4:18).

Through his new tutor, Caspian has the opportunity to learn the truth—and to choose a different path than his "grandcesters." This is a choice every believer must make. Ephesians 5 explains, "You were once darkness, but now you are light in the Lord. Live as children of light . . . in all goodness, righteousness and truth and find out what pleases the Lord. Have nothing to do with the fruitless deeds of darkness, but rather expose them. . . . Be very careful . . . how you live—not as unwise, but as wise, making the most of every opportunity, because the days are evil" (vv. 8-11, 15-16).

Do You Know?

According to wise, old Doctor Cornelius, the meeting of the stars Tarva and Alambil means "great good for the sad realm of Narnia." Some wise men in the Bible believed that the appearance of a particular star meant that something good was about to happen in Israel. Do you know what it was?

(Hint: Read Matthew 2:1-12.)

Scriptures on Keeping Your Mouth Shut

Proverbs 11:13   Proverbs 12:23   Proverbs 13:3

5. CASPIAN'S ADVENTURE IN THE MOUNTAINS

Deliver me, O my God, from the hand of the wicked, from the grasp of evil and cruel men. For you have been my hope, O Sovereign LORD, my confidence since my youth. PSALM 71:4-5

Biblical Parallels and Principles

‷ Over Nikabrik's objections, Trumpkin and Trufflehunter insist on showing kindness to Caspian. The Scripture is full of admonitions such as these: "Share with God's people who are in need" (Romans 12:13). "The alien living with you must be treated as one of your native-born. Love him as yourself" (Leviticus 19:34). "Offer hospitality to one another without grumbling" (1 Peter 4:9). "Do not forget to entertain strangers, for by so doing some people have entertained angels without knowing it" (Hebrews 13:2).

‷ It has been over a thousand years since the Golden Age of Narnia. Nikabrik and Trumpkin have as much trouble believing the stories of Aslan and the Kings and Queens as some people in our time have trouble believing the Bible. The Scripture tells us, "Faith is being sure of what we hope for and certain of what we do not see" (Hebrews 11:1). Trufflehunter shows the faith Jesus commended in John 20:29, where we read that Jesus said to His disciples, "Because you have seen me, you have believed; blessed are those who have not seen and yet have believed."

Do You Know?

No matter what the others think, Trufflehunter says that he will be faithful to Aslan and the King. He is a true disciple: "We don't change, we beasts. We don't forget." The Bible tells us about Someone who never forgets and never changes and who always remains faithful. Do you know who?

(Hint: Read Hebrews 13:8 and 2 Timothy 2:11-13.)

Scriptures on Faith

2 Corinthians 5:7   Hebrews 11   Romans 1:16-17

6. THE PEOPLE THAT LIVED IN HIDING

When the wicked rise to power, people go into hiding; but when the wicked perish, the righteous thrive. PROVERBS 28:28

Biblical Parallels and Principles

🔖 Caspian is shocked to realize that the horrible creatures from the old stories are just as real as the nice ones. Many people find it pleasant to believe in the existence of guardian angels. But if we believe the Bible is true, we have to realize that the spirit world is not only inhabited by angels but also by demons. We have a loving Heavenly Father who cares for us; we also have an enemy who seeks to "devour" us (1 Peter 5:8)! That's why Ephesians 6:11-12 says, "Put on the full armor of God so that you can take your stand against the devil's schemes. For our struggle is not against flesh and blood, but against . . . the powers of this dark world and against the spiritual forces of evil in the heavenly realms."

🔖 Nikabrik will believe in anyone or anything that will drive the Telmarines out of Narnia. Some of Jesus' followers felt the same way. They would believe in anyone they thought could deliver them from Roman oppression. They wanted to make Jesus their king, but when they realized that He wasn't about to lead a military revolt, they abandoned Him (John 6:15, 66). Scripture tells us that in times of trouble, instead of calling on Him, God's people repeatedly made alliances with heathen nations, worshiped false gods, and appealed to evil spirits for help (Isaiah 30:1-2; 31:1). The results were always disastrous.

Do You Know?

To his delight, Caspian discovers that there are many Old Narnians still living—they've just been in hiding. During the reign of a wicked king, a prophet complained that he was the only servant of God still living in the land—until God told him there were seven thousand others! Many of them were just in hiding. Do you remember the prophet's name?

(Hint: Read 1 Kings 19:14-18; see also 1 Kings 18:4.)

Scriptures on Hiding in God

Psalm 17:6-9   Psalm 32:7   Psalm 143:9

7. OLD NARNIA IN DANGER

*The night is nearly over; the day is almost here. So let us put
aside the deeds of darkness and put on the armor of light.*

ROMANS 13:12

Biblical Parallels and Principles

❧ At the council of war, Caspian listens to the wisdom and guidance of
Doctor Cornelius, Glenstorm, Trufflehunter, and the others. Proverbs
20:18 says, "Make plans by seeking advice; if you wage war, obtain guidance." And Proverbs 11:14 observes, "For lack of guidance a nation falls,
but many advisers make victory sure."

❧ Caspian decides to use Queen Susan's horn to summon help. In the
Scriptures, the sound of the horn called soldiers to battle. It was a cry for
help. The horn also symbolized power and strength and deliverance. (See
2 Samuel 22:3; Psalm 89:16-17, 24; 112:9.) Zechariah prophesied about
the coming of the Messiah (Jesus) in Luke 1:67-75: "Praise be to the
Lord. . . . He has raised up a horn of salvation for us . . . to rescue us from
the hand of our enemies, and to enable us to serve him without fear in
holiness and righteousness before him all our days."

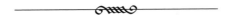

Sound Familiar?

Aslan's How is a sacred memorial mound, built like a tomb over the ruins
of the Stone Table. Inside are tunnels and caves, all lined with stones that
form mosaics. Many feature a lion or some other ancient and mysterious
symbol. When the early church suffered persecution from the Roman
emperors, they went underground—building miles of caves and tunnels and
passages called catacombs. They used the catacombs as a secret refuge, a place
to meet for worship and prayer, and a place to bury their loved ones.
Archaeologists have found these tunnels lined with mosaics depicting scenes
from the life of Christ, as well as doves, fish, and other Christian symbols.

Scriptures on Persevering in Battle

Romans 8:31-37   Psalm 18:32-39   1 Timothy 6:12

8. HOW THEY LEFT THE ISLAND

Be merciful to those who doubt. JUDE 22

Biblical Parallels and Principles

⁂ The children realize that they did not stumble into Narnia by accident—they have been called. The Bible tells us that all believers are called by God to fulfill His plans and purposes here on earth: "You are a chosen people, a royal priesthood, a holy nation, a people belonging to God, that you may declare the praises of him who called you out of darkness into his wonderful light" (1 Peter 2:9).

⁂ Trumpkin can't see how four children could possibly help Narnia. First Corinthians 1:26-27 says, "Brothers, think of what you were when you were called. Not many of you were wise by human standards; not many were influential; not many were of noble birth. But God chose the foolish things of the world to shame the wise; God chose the weak things of the world to shame the strong."

⁂ Each of the children takes turns demonstrating his or her abilities and talents—and the unique gifts Aslan has given him or her. The Bible tells us that all believers have received gifts from God. These gifts include wisdom, knowledge, administration, faith, healing, miracles, prophecy, and discernment (1 Corinthians 12:8-11, 28-31). We are to use our gifts to help one another, strengthen one another, and build up the Body of Christ. "If one part suffers, every part suffers with it; if one part is honored, every part rejoices with it" (1 Corinthians 12:26).

Do You Know?

Trumpkin says he believes the children, but he doesn't really understand who they are and what they are able to do. Some of Jesus' disciples had the same problem. How did Jesus demonstrate His power to them?

(Hint: Read Matthew 14:22-33.)

Scriptures on Doubt

Matthew 13:57-58   James 1:5-8   Matthew 21:18-22

9. WHAT LUCY SAW

Let your eyes look straight ahead, fix your gaze directly before you. Make level paths for your feet and take only ways that are firm. PROVERBS 4:25-26

Biblical Parallels and Principles

Seeing the wild bear, Lucy begins to wonder what might happen if, here in our world, "men started going wild inside." The Scripture tells us that is exactly what has happened—and will continue to happen as human history draws to a close: "There will be terrible times in the last days. People will be . . . abusive . . . unholy . . . without self-control, brutal . . . treacherous, rash, conceited, lovers of pleasure rather than lovers of God" (2 Timothy 3:1-5). Romans 1:28-29 says, "Furthermore, since they did not think it worthwhile to retain the knowledge of God, he gave them over to a depraved mind, to do what ought not to be done. They have become filled with every kind of wickedness, evil, greed and depravity." (See also Romans 1:18-32; Jude 10.)

Lucy is heartbroken that no one believes her. They all insist that she can't have seen Aslan. A young woman named Mary Magdalene was the first to see Jesus after His death and resurrection. "She went and told those who had been with him. . . . When they heard that Jesus was alive and that she had seen him, they did not believe it" (Mark 16:10-11; see also Luke 24:10-11).

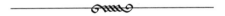

Do You Know?

In *The Lion, the Witch and the Wardrobe*, Edmund teased Lucy mercilessly about her "imaginary" country—only to discover that her story was true. He has learned from his experience. Where he had been proud and arrogant, he is now humble and thoughtful. What does the Bible say comes with humility?

(Hint: Read Proverbs 11:2.)

Scriptures on Finding the Right Path

Psalm 16:11   Proverbs 3:5-6   Psalm 23:1-4

10. THE RETURN OF THE LION

Seek the LORD while he may be found; call on him while he is near. ISAIAH 55:6

Biblical Parallels and Principles

꘠ Aslan says he seems bigger to Lucy because she is older. Usually the opposite is true: As we grow bigger, we discover the things that seemed so big to us before are actually *smaller* than we remember them. Not so with God. The bigger we get, the more we realize how truly big He is, how small we are, and how much we still have to learn. In Ephesians 3:17-19 the apostle Paul said, "I pray that you, being rooted and established in love, may have power, together with all the saints, to grasp how wide and long and high and deep is the love of Christ . . . that you may be filled to the measure of all the fullness of God."

꘠ Lucy feels sorry for herself at the thought of the unpleasant task before her. But Aslan reminds her that "it has been hard for us all in Narnia before now." Others have suffered so much more. In 1 Peter 5:9, battle-weary believers are encouraged to keep resisting the devil and stand firm in their faith "because you know that your brothers throughout the world are undergoing the same kind of sufferings."

꘠ Aslan tells Lucy that if the others don't believe her, it doesn't matter: "You at least must follow me alone." Throughout His earthly ministry, Jesus called people to leave their homes, their families, their businesses—to sacrifice everything—to follow Him. He warned His disciples that their own brothers and sisters would turn against them because of Him (Luke 12:51-53). When the disciples asked what God would require of others, Jesus replied, "What is that to you? You must follow me" (John 21:22).

Do You Know?

Lucy has a very special relationship with Aslan. Because she follows him wholeheartedly, she draws closer to him and learns to know him better than some of the others do. One of Jesus' disciples was especially close to His heart. Do you remember who?

(Hint: Read John 13:22-25; 21:24. Four books of the New Testament bear his name.)

Scriptures on the Difference Between God's Ways and Our Own

Isaiah 55:8-9   1 Corinthians 2:10-14   Romans 11:33-36

11. THE LION ROARS

The hour has come for you to wake up from your slumber,
because our salvation is nearer now than when we first believed.

ROMANS 13:11

Biblical Parallels and Principles

֍ Regardless of what the others say or do, Lucy knows she must obey Aslan—she must follow him. First Peter 3:14-16 tells us how we should respond to similar situations in our lives: "Even if you should suffer for what is right, you are blessed. 'Do not fear what they fear; do not be frightened.' But in your hearts set apart Christ as Lord. Always be prepared to give an answer to everyone who asks you to give the reason for the hope that you have. But do this with gentleness and respect, keeping a clear conscience, so that those who speak maliciously against your good behavior in Christ may be ashamed of their slander."

֍ Lucy forgot everything—her fears and her frustrations with Susan—when she "fixed her eyes on Aslan." Hebrews 12:1-3 says, "Since we are surrounded by such a great cloud of witnesses, let us throw off everything that hinders and the sin that so easily entangles, and let us run with perseverance the race marked out for us. Let us fix our eyes on Jesus, the author and perfecter of our faith, who for the joy set before him endured the cross, scorning its shame, and sat down at the right hand of the throne of God. Consider him who endured such opposition from sinful men, so that you will not grow weary and lose heart."

֍ Aslan leads the children right through the gorge—along secret paths and hidden ledges they failed to discover on their own. In Isaiah 42:16 God says, "I will lead the blind by ways they have not known, along unfamiliar paths I will guide them; I will turn the darkness into light before them and make the rough places smooth. These are the things I will do; I will not forsake them."

֍ Aslan tells Susan that she has "listened to [her] fears." In her guilt and shame, she can barely face him. First John 3:16-20 reminds us to focus on God's love for us, as expressed by Jesus' death on the cross: "This is how . . . we set our hearts at rest in his presence whenever our hearts condemn us. For God is greater than our hearts, and he knows everything." Aslan breathes on Susan, just as Jesus breathed on His frightened disciples (John 20:22), and reassures her of his love. First John 4:18 tells us, "There is no fear in love, but perfect love casts out fear" (ESV).

🕸 Aslan greets Edmund with the words, "Well done." In Matthew 25:21 Jesus described how God responds to our obedience to Him: "Well done, good and faithful servant! You have been faithful with a few things; I will put you in charge of many things. Come and share your master's happiness!"

🕸 In spite of their lack of sleep, Peter and Edmund show no signs of weariness. Being in Aslan's presence has refreshed them. Isaiah 40:29-31 tells us that God "gives strength to the weary and increases the power of the weak. Even youths grow tired and weary, and young men stumble and fall; but those who hope in the LORD will renew their strength. They will soar on wings like eagles; they will run and not grow weary, they will walk and not faint."

Do You Know?

Susan and Lucy once again witness Aslan's miraculous deliverance of Narnia. They participate in a fantastic celebration—singing, dancing, and feasting. Do you know who or what the Bible says will enjoy "a continual feast"?

(Hint: Read Proverbs 15:15.)

Scriptures on Persevering in Times of Testing

Philippians 3:7-14   James 1:2-4   Hebrews 12:4-13

12. SORCERY AND SUDDEN VENGEANCE

Woe to those who call evil good and good evil, who put darkness for light and light for darkness. ISAIAH 5:20

Biblical Parallels and Principles

◈ Nikabrik insists that no help has come, but Trufflehunter says prophetically, "It may even now be at the door." The badger's faith is like that of the psalmist who said, "I am still confident of this: I will see the goodness of the LORD in the land of the living" (Psalm 27:13). Isaiah 30:18 tells us, "The LORD longs to be gracious to you; he rises to show you compassion. For the LORD is a God of justice. Blessed are all who wait for him!"

◈ Nikabrik questions the truth of the old stories, suggesting that Aslan never rose from the dead and that much of what Narnians have believed is nothing more than myth or fairy tale. Since the cross, unbelievers have brought those same accusations against Christians. Matthew 28:11-15 tells us how the soldiers who witnessed Jesus' resurrection conspired to say that He did not rise from the dead, that His disciples merely stole His body: "And this story has been widely circulated . . . to this day." But the apostle Peter insisted, "We did not follow cleverly invented stories when we told you about the power and coming of our Lord Jesus Christ, but we were eyewitnesses of his majesty" (2 Peter 1:16).

◈ When Nikabrik suggests that they summon the White Witch, Caspian responds with righteous anger. In the Scriptures, God absolutely forbids necromancy—the attempt to contact the spirits of the dead. Isaiah 8:19 says, "When men tell you to consult mediums and spiritists, who whisper and mutter, should not a people inquire of their God? Why consult the dead on behalf of the living?" Deuteronomy 18:10-12 tells us, "Anyone who does these things is detestable to the LORD."

◈ Though he had never seen Aslan himself, and though stories of the Kings and Queens were a thousand years old, still Trufflehunter persisted in his faith. In 1 Peter 1:8-9 the apostle Peter speaks to those of us who did not have the opportunity to walk with Jesus as he and the other disciples did and yet still believe: "Though you have not seen him, you love him; and even though you do not see him now, you believe in him and are filled with an inexpressible and glorious joy, for you are receiving the goal of your faith, the salvation of your souls." One day, like Trufflehunter, we will have the privilege of meeting the One in whom we have believed—the King of kings—face to face.

Do You Know?

For years Nikabrik allowed hatred and bitterness to fill his heart, until it consumed him. What does the Bible tell us to do with those emotions?

(Hint: Read Ephesians 4:31—5:2.)

Scriptures on Waiting for God's Deliverance

Psalm 33:20-22   Lamentations 3:22-26   Romans 8:18-25

13. THE HIGH KING IN COMMAND

The integrity of the upright guides them, but the unfaithful are destroyed by their duplicity. PROVERBS 11:3

Biblical Parallels and Principles

❧ Peter observes that Aslan acts "in his time . . . not ours." The Scripture often uses phrases such as "in the fullness of time" or "at the appointed time" to indicate that everything happens just as God ordains—according to His plan and His timetable. "With the Lord a day is like a thousand years, and a thousand years are like a day" (2 Peter 3:8). We don't always understand the delay, but 2 Peter 3:9 assures us that "the Lord is not slow in keeping his promise, as some understand slowness. He is patient." According to Ecclesiastes 3:11, "He has made everything beautiful in its time."

❧ "A kind of greatness" has hung about Edmund since his encounter with Aslan. The Bible tells us that after Moses met with God on Mount Sinai, his face shone so brightly that he had to wear a veil (Exodus 34:29-33). Second Corinthians 3:18 says that now all believers, with unveiled faces, "reflect the Lord's glory." Acts 4:13 tells us that the disciples were put on trial, and when the people "saw the courage of Peter and John and realized that they were unschooled, ordinary men, they were astonished and they took note that these men had been with Jesus."

❧ Miraz has surrounded himself with evil men—the kind who would support his murderous plans and aid him in his treachery. But he is foolish to make such men his counselors. Proverbs 12:5 warns, "The advice of the wicked is deceitful." Proverbs 26:24-25 explains, "A malicious man disguises himself with his lips, but in his heart he harbors deceit. Though his speech is charming, do not believe him, for seven abominations fill his heart."

Sound Familiar?

Peter begins his challenge to Miraz by referring to his position as High King "by the gift of Aslan." (The phrase at once asserts his authority: Aslan appointed him and put him in charge. At the same time, it is a humble acknowledgment that his power comes from Aslan and not from himself.) One of the early church leaders began nearly all of his letters the same way, referring to himself as an apostle appointed by Jesus Christ. Do you know who?

(Hint: Read Galatians 1:1; see also Romans 1:1; 1 and 2 Corinthians 1:1; Ephesians 1:1; Colossians 1:1; 1 and 2 Timothy 1:1; and Titus 1:1.)

Scriptures on the Ways of the Wise

Proverbs 14:29   Proverbs 17:27   Proverbs 19:11

14. HOW ALL WERE VERY BUSY

When justice is done, it brings joy to the righteous but terror to evildoers. PROVERBS 21:15

Biblical Parallels and Principles

⅋ Almost before the Narnians are "really warmed to their work," the Telmarines are defeated. In Exodus 23:27 God promised, "I will send my terror ahead of you and throw into confusion every nation you encounter. I will make all your enemies turn their backs and run."

⅋ Once again Aslan brings deliverance to Narnia, setting the captives free (compare Isaiah 61:1). Jeremiah 31:11-13 describes how God will deliver His people: "For the LORD will . . . redeem them from the hand of those stronger than they. They will come and shout for joy on the heights of Zion; they will rejoice in the bounty of the LORD—the grain, the new wine and the oil, the young of the flocks and herds. They will be like a well-watered garden, and they will sorrow no more. Then maidens will dance and be glad, young men and old as well. I will turn their mourning into gladness; I will give them comfort and joy instead of sorrow."

⅋ Aslan not only delivers Old Narnia, but he rescues Telmarines whose hearts are tender toward him. Jesus made it clear that He did not come to save only one race or people (John 10:16; 1 John 2:2). Revelation 5:9 tells us that with His blood, He has purchased or redeemed men "from every tribe and language and people and nation." In Revelation 3:20 Jesus issued an open invitation: "Here I am! I stand at the door and knock. If anyone hears my voice and opens the door, I will come in . . ."

Sound Familiar?

Bacchus hands Caspian's old nurse a pitcher of water from the well. Upon tasting it, she discovers that it has been turned to wine! Someone in the Bible offered the thirsty "a spring of water welling up to eternal life," and His first miracle was turning water into wine. Do you know who it was?

(Hint: Read John 4:13-14 and John 2:7-11.)

Scriptures on Celebrating God's Victory

Exodus 15:1-13   Psalm 148   Revelation 11:17-18

15. ASLAN MAKES A DOOR IN THE AIR

This day I call heaven and earth as witnesses . . . that I have set before you life and death, blessings and curses. Now choose life, so that you and your children may live and that you may love the LORD your God and listen to his voice, and hold fast to him. For the LORD is your life. DEUTERONOMY 30:19-20

Biblical Parallels and Principles

꿩 Aslan tells Caspian that if he had felt himself sufficient, it would have been proof that he was not. Romans 12:3 tells us, "Do not think of yourselves more highly than you ought." And 1 Corinthians 10:12 says, "If you think you are standing firm, be careful that you don't fall!" The apostle Paul urged believers to "put no confidence in the flesh" (Philippians 3:3). Instead, we should recognize our human frailty and our total dependence on God. "He [God] said to me, 'My grace is sufficient for you, for my power is made perfect in weakness.' Therefore I will boast all the more gladly about my weaknesses, so that Christ's power may rest on me" (2 Corinthians 12:9-10).

꿩 Reepicheep's friends bring him to Aslan for healing. In Luke 5:18-26 some friends brought a paralyzed man to Jesus. When they couldn't get in at the door because of the crowds, they lowered him through the roof on a mat. Jesus was moved when He "saw their faith." For the sake of his friends, He healed the man.

꿩 Lucy has a special relationship with Aslan; she loves him wholeheartedly and serves him faithfully. At the feast she is "sitting close" to him—a picture of devotion. The Scriptures describe the same devotion in Mary of Bethany, who sat at Jesus' feet (Luke 10:39), and in John the Beloved, who leaned back against Jesus at the Last Supper (John 13:25).

꿩 Aslan "feasted the Narnians" all day and all night. Throughout His earthly ministry, Jesus fed His disciples, sometimes four or five thousand at a time (Matthew 14:13-21; 15:29-38)! In His parables, He often used banquets and feasts to describe the kingdom of God (Matthew 22:1-14; Luke 14:15-23). Jesus promised that one day all believers will join Him for a magnificent celebration in Heaven—"the wedding supper of the Lamb" (Revelation 19:9).

115

❧ Caspian learns that being a Son of Adam or Daughter of Eve is both an honor and a shame. It is an honor to be unique among all Creation—"created . . . in the image of God" (Genesis 1:27; also see 2:7). But it is a shame to be responsible for bringing sin and death into the world. "Through the disobedience of the one man the many were made sinners" (Romans 5:19).

Sound Familiar?

Susan and Lucy are very similar to two sisters in the Bible. One—like Susan—was focused on "practical things," while the other—like Lucy—focused on "spiritual things." Do you remember the sisters' names?

(Hint: Read Luke 10:38-42.)

Scriptures on Life-changing Choices

Joshua 24:14-15   John 3:16-18   John 15:16

THE VOYAGE
OF THE
DAWN TREADER

Introduction to

The Voyage of the Dawn Treader

By this time either they had grown much smaller or the picture had grown bigger. Eustace jumped to try to pull it off the wall and found himself standing on the frame; in front of him was not glass but real sea, and wind and waves rushing right up to the frame as they might to a rock. He lost his head and clutched at the other two who had jumped up beside him. There was a second of struggling and shouting, and just as they thought they had got their balance a great blue roller surged up round them, swept them off their feet, and drew them down into the sea.

THE VOYAGE OF THE DAWN TREADER

After falling through a picture in England, Edmund and Lucy and their cousin Eustace suddenly find themselves sailing aboard the *Dawn Treader* in the Great Eastern Ocean off the coast of Narnia. It's been three years in Narnian time since the Pevensies' last adventure. The land is at peace; all is well. And so King Caspian has begun a quest to find the Seven Lords who disappeared from Narnia during his evil uncle's reign. Reepicheep, the Chief Mouse, has a higher hope—a greater ambition: "Why should we not come to the very eastern end of the world? And what might we find there? I expect to find Aslan's country."

The Voyage of the Dawn Treader is a series of adventures, a story of many spiritual journeys. For Caspian, Edmund, and Lucy, it is a journey of spiritual maturity. They will have numerous opportunities to put into practice the admonition of Romans 12:9-21: "Hate what is evil; cling to what is good. Be devoted to one another in brotherly love. Honor one another above yourselves. Never be lacking in zeal, but keep your spiritual fervor, serving the Lord. Be joyful in hope, patient in affliction, faithful in prayer. Share with God's people who are in need. Practice hospitality. . . . Rejoice with those who rejoice; mourn with those who mourn. . . . Do not be overcome by evil, but overcome evil with good."

For Reepicheep, the voyage is the climax or culmination of the journey of his life. He has "fought the good fight" (2 Timothy 4:7), and now his eyes are firmly fixed on eternity. Soon he will experience the fulfillment of his lifelong dream—to be in Aslan's country (Heaven). He can wait no longer. "My soul yearns, even faints, for the courts of the LORD; my heart and my flesh cry out for the living God" (Psalm 84:2).

For Eustace, it's a journey of transformation. He arrives in Narnia as a mean, selfish, obnoxious child who makes life miserable for everyone on board the ship. But when Eustace is transformed into a dragon, the scales fall from his eyes (compare Acts 9:18). He sees himself for the miserable sinner that he is and realizes his need for a Savior. In one of the most powerful illustrations of a conversion experience in *The Chronicles*, Aslan comes to Eustace's rescue and releases him from the imprisonment of his dragon self. Eustace literally casts off the outer man—the old nature, the flesh—to become a new creature (see 2 Corinthians 5:17). "He began to be a different boy."

When he wrote *The Voyage of the Dawn Treader*, C.S. Lewis thought he was completing *The Chronicles of Narnia*. There is clearly a sense of finality. The journey comes to a close at the shores of Aslan's country, and the Pevensie children are told that their adventures in Narnia have come to an end. In the very last scene Lewis makes the most explicit reference to the "story within the story" and the purpose for his writing *The Chronicles*. Aslan tells the children that although they will not meet him in Narnia again, they can know him in their own world: "But there I have another name. You must learn to know me by that name. This was the very reason why you were brought to Narnia, that by knowing me here for a little, you may know me better there."

You will discover this and many other spiritual treasures as you embark on *The Voyage of the Dawn Treader*.

1. THE PICTURE IN THE BEDROOM

He reached down from on high and took hold of me; he drew me out of deep waters. PSALM 18:16

Biblical Parallels and Principles

Readers in C.S. Lewis's day would recognize the description of Harold and Alberta's lifestyle as mirroring all the latest "modern," "scientific" approaches to parenting and healthy living. In subscribing to all the latest ideas, they have discarded old-fashioned values such as courtesy and respect for others. There is no warmth or comfort in their home, no room for faith or hope or imagination. Colossians 2:8 warns believers, "See to it that no one takes you captive through hollow and deceptive philosophy, which depends on human tradition and the basic principles of this world rather than on Christ."

Although Eustace's words are extremely offensive, Reepicheep restrains himself. Proverbs 12:16 says, "A fool shows his annoyance at once, but a prudent man overlooks an insult."

Unlike Eustace, Lucy is thrilled to be aboard ship, "quite sure they were in for a lovely time." Proverbs 15:15 tells us, "The cheerful heart has a continual feast."

Do You Know?

Eustace says many mean and spiteful things—and it seems he has no control over his tongue. The Bible compares the tongue to a part of a ship. Do you know which part?

(Hint: Read James 3:4-5.)

Scriptures on the Lord of the Sea

Psalm 93   Psalm 104:24-26   Psalm 135:6

2. ON BOARD THE *DAWN TREADER*

Be prepared in season and out of season; correct, rebuke and encourage—with great patience and careful instruction. 2 TIMOTHY 4:2

Biblical Parallels and Principles

🔖 Reepicheep has a deep longing to travel east to Aslan's country. The psalmist expressed a similar desire: "How lovely is your dwelling place, O LORD Almighty! My soul yearns, even faints, for the courts of the LORD; my heart and my flesh cry out for the living God. . . . Better is one day in your courts than a thousand elsewhere" (Psalm 84:1-2, 10).

🔖 Caspian, Edmund, and Lucy demonstrate the maturity that all believers are called to in Romans 12:10-16: "Be devoted to one another in brotherly love. Honor one another above yourselves. . . . Be joyful in hope, patient in affliction, faithful in prayer. . . . Practice hospitality. Bless those who persecute you. . . . Live in harmony with one another."

🔖 Eustace has never received corporal punishment before—and it has quite an impact on him! Proverbs 22:15 says, "Folly is bound up in the heart of a child, but the rod of discipline will drive it far from him." (See also Proverbs 13:24; 23:13-14.)

Do You Know?

Caspian wisely made his vow to search for the Seven Lords "with Aslan's approval." What does the Bible say about making a vow or an oath?

(Hint: Read Ecclesiastes 5:2, 4-5.)

Scriptures on Correction and Discipline

Proverbs 12:1   Proverbs 15:32   Psalm 94:12

3. THE LONE ISLANDS

"For I will surely show you kindness for the sake of your father."

2 SAMUEL 9:7

Biblical Parallels and Principles

Governor Gumpas does everything in the king's name, but he would "not be pleased to find a real, live King of Narnia coming in upon him." Jesus warned believers that not everyone who does things in His name is truly His faithful servant. Many of these will not enter the Kingdom of Heaven. Jesus said, "I will tell them plainly, 'I never knew you. Away from me, you evildoers'" (Matthew 7:23).

Lord Bern warns Caspian that Governor Gumpas would not deny allegiance to the crown, but he would pretend not to believe that Caspian was who he claimed to be—and he would seek to have him killed. In Luke 20:9-16 Jesus told a parable in which some unfaithful tenants did exactly that to the landowner's son. (Jesus was prophesying what the religious leaders would do to Him: They would claim allegiance to God but reject Him as God's Son and have Him crucified.)

Although he is the king, Caspian is willing to receive Lord Bern's counsel. Proverbs 19:20 says, "Listen to advice and accept instruction, and in the end you will be wise." Proverbs 15:22 observes, "Plans fail for lack of counsel, but with many advisers they succeed."

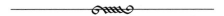

Sound Familiar?

Caspian wants to keep his identity a secret for the time being. The Bible tells us about a King who did not always want His identity revealed. Do you know who?

(Hint: Read Mark 3:11-12; 8:27-30.)

Scriptures on Spiritual Slavery

Proverbs 5:22   2 Peter 2:17-19   John 8:34-36

4. WHAT CASPIAN DID THERE

"Therefore keep watch, because you do not know on what day your Lord will come." MATTHEW 24:42

Biblical Parallels and Principles

꙰ Gumpas is completely caught off guard by Caspian's arrival. Jesus told His disciples to be alert and watch for His Second Coming. In His absence they were to remain faithful to all He had taught them: "Who then is the faithful and wise servant, whom the master has put in charge of the servants of his household to give them their food at the proper time? It will be good for that servant whose master finds him doing so when he returns" (Matthew 24:45-46). The unfaithful servant who abuses his power and privilege had better watch out: "The master of that servant will come on a day when he does not expect him and at an hour he is not aware of" (v. 50). He will be severely punished.

꙰ Caspian removes the disloyal, dishonest governor and installs Lord Bern in his place. In the Parable of the Talents, Jesus warned that those who are irresponsible and unfaithful will lose their position. What they have will be taken from them and will be given to those who are worthy and faithful (Matthew 25:28-29).

꙰ Caspian puts an end to the evils of slave trade in the Lone Islands. The Bible does not specifically forbid slavery; it was a common practice in almost every culture. Some slaves were prisoners of war; others sold themselves or their family members into slavery for a period of time, in order to pay off debts. The Scripture does forbid kidnapping and then making those kidnapped into slaves (Exodus 21:16; Deuteronomy 24:7). According to the Law, slaves were to be treated with dignity and respect. Provisions were made for them to earn or receive their freedom (Exodus 21:2-11; Leviticus 25:35-55; Deuteronomy 15:12-18). In the New Testament, the apostle Paul said that slaves and slave owners had equal standing in the kingdom of God—as brothers in Christ (Galatians 3:28; Philemon 12-16; Ephesians 6:5-9). Jesus came to "proclaim freedom for the prisoners" and to "release the oppressed" (Luke 4:17-21). Slave traders are included in a list of godless, immoral people found in 1 Timothy 1:9-10, right along with liars, murderers, and adulterers.

Sound Familiar?

On his journey to Aslan's country, Caspian stops to clean house, ridding the Lone Islands of vice and corruption and restoring order to the colonies. In a symbolic gesture, the governor's table is overturned, and all his official letters and papers are swept away. The Bible tells us about Someone who overturned tables as He cleaned out the robbery and corruption in His house. Do you know who?

(Hint: Read Matthew 21:12-13.)

Scriptures on Faithful Stewardship

Luke 16:10   Matthew 25:14-30   3 John 3-7

5. THE STORM AND WHAT CAME OF IT

An unfriendly man pursues selfish ends; he defies all sound judgment. PROVERBS 18:1

Biblical Parallels and Principles

Eustace is so self-absorbed that he thinks of no one and nothing else. He whines and complains constantly. He is completely blind to his own faults, reacting bitterly to any attempt to encourage or instruct him. Proverbs 15:12 observes, "A mocker resents correction; he will not consult the wise." Ephesians 4:18 says such people are "darkened in their understanding and separated from the life of God because of the ignorance that is in them due to the hardening of their hearts."

Eustace has done nothing to deserve Lucy's kindness, but Lucy is kind anyway. "If your enemy is hungry, give him food to eat; if he is thirsty, give him water to drink" (Proverbs 25:21). First Peter 3:9 says, "Do not repay evil with evil or insult with insult, but with blessing." Ephesians 4:2 tells believers, "Be completely humble and gentle; be patient, bearing with one another in love." In Matthew 5:7 Jesus observes, "Blessed are the merciful, for they will be shown mercy."

Do You Know?

The *Dawn Treader* barely survived a fierce storm that lasted twelve days. The Bible tells us that one of the apostles was shipwrecked after a storm that raged on for fourteen days. Do you know which apostle?

(Hint: Read Acts 27:13-44.)

Scriptures on the One Who Stills Storms

Psalm 89:8-9   Psalm 107:28-30   Matthew 8:23-27

6. THE ADVENTURES OF EUSTACE

*Your gold and silver are corroded. Their corrosion will testify
against you and eat your flesh like fire. You have hoarded wealth.*

JAMES 5:3

Biblical Parallels and Principles

Being transformed into a dragon causes Eustace to see himself for who he really is. At last his eyes have been opened. The psalmist said, "My guilt has overwhelmed me like a burden too heavy to bear. . . . I am bowed down and brought very low . . . feeble and utterly crushed; I groan in anguish of heart. . . . My heart pounds, my strength fails me; even the light has gone from my eyes. My friends and companions avoid me" (Psalm 38:4, 6, 8, 10-11). In Romans 7:24 the apostle Paul exclaimed, "What a wretched man I am! Who will rescue me from this body of death?"

Caspian and the others are cautious in approaching the dragon, wary of what may be a trick. Proverbs 14:15 says, "A simple man believes anything, but a prudent man gives thought to his steps." Jesus told His disciples to be "wise as serpents, and harmless as doves" (Matthew 10:16, KJV). First Peter 5:8 warns, "Be self-controlled and alert. Your enemy the devil prowls around . . . looking for someone to devour."

Think About It!

Eustace had read "none of the right books" and did not immediately recognize the dragon for what it was. Every culture in the world has stories and legends about dragons. In the book of Revelation, the dragon is a symbol of Satan. There are many other references to dragons in the Bible, but some versions translate the word as "serpent" or "jackal," depending on the context. Then there are the fire-breathing "leviathan" (Job 3:8; 41; Psalm 74:14; 104:26; Isaiah 27:1) and the mighty "behemoth" (Job 40:15-24) that once roamed the earth. Early cultures referred to these creatures as dragons and sea monsters. Creation scientists believe they were what we would call dinosaurs.

Scriptures on Greed

Ecclesiastes 5:10   Luke 12:15   1 Timothy 6:9-10

7. HOW THE ADVENTURE ENDED

Come, let us return to the LORD. He has torn us to pieces but he will heal us; he has injured us but he will bind up our wounds.
HOSEA 6:1

Biblical Parallels and Principles

In spite of Eustace's antagonism toward him, Reepicheep has consistently treated Eustace with courtesy and respect. In Eustace's hour of need, Reepicheep is his most faithful friend and companion. In Matthew 5:44 Jesus told His disciples, "Love your enemies and pray for those who persecute you." Proverbs 25:21 says, "If your enemy is hungry, give him food to eat; if he is thirsty, give him water to drink." By doing so, we may be able to win others over and rescue them from judgment (1 Peter 3:1; 1 Corinthians 9:19; Jude 23).

Eustace's encounter with Aslan illustrates many of the fundamental truths of our salvation or conversion experience. We do not seek God, but He seeks us (Romans 3:10-11; Luke 19:10). We needed a Savior because we were helpless, unable to save ourselves (Romans 5:6-8). None of our efforts made any difference (Isaiah 64:6; Ephesians 2:8-9; Titus 3:5). When we realized our condition—the depth of our sin—we were cut to the heart (Acts 2:37-38; Psalm 38:4). God removed all the layers of sin and filth and wickedness (Romans 6:6; 1 John 1:9). He cleansed us (Titus 3:5; Ephesians 5:25b-27), baptized us (1 Peter 3:21; Colossians 2:10, 12), and clothed us with His righteousness (Isaiah 61:10). We have become new creations (2 Corinthians 5:17). We are born again (John 3:3-6). In Ezekiel 36:26 God said, "I will give you a new heart and put a new spirit in you; I will remove from you your heart of stone and give you a heart of flesh."

Edmund answers the question, "Do you know him?" by saying, "Well—he knows me." We know God a little, but He is so far beyond our human comprehension. Only in Heaven will we be able to grasp all that He is. "Now we see but a poor reflection as in a mirror; then we shall see face to face. Now I know in part; then I shall know fully, even as I am fully known" (1 Corinthians 13:12). According to Psalm 139:1-16, God knows *us* inside out. "For you created my inmost being; you knit me together in my mother's womb" (v. 13).

Do You Know?

Although there was no moon, Eustace says, "there was moonlight where the lion was." The Bible tells us there will be no need for sunlight or moonlight in Heaven. Do you know why?

    (Hint: Read Revelation 21:23; 22:5.)

Scriptures on Becoming a New Creation in Christ

2 Corinthians 5:17   Colossians 2:6-7   2 Peter 1:5-11

8. TWO NARROW ESCAPES

Our God is a God who saves; from the Sovereign LORD comes escape from death. PSALM 68:20

Biblical Parallels and Principles

☙ Caspian is overcome by a desire for the wealth and power that the gold water may bring him. He binds everyone to secrecy as he plans to claim and acquire this new wealth. Proverbs 14:12 observes, "There is a way that seems right to a man, but in the end it leads to death." First Timothy 6:9 explains, "People who want to get rich fall into temptation and a trap and into many foolish and harmful desires that plunge men into ruin and destruction." Jesus warned His disciples, "Watch out! Be on your guard against all kinds of greed; a man's life does not consist in the abundance of his possessions" (Luke 12:15).

☙ Aslan suddenly appears at a crucial moment. His presence banishes every evil thought and brings everyone to their senses. "The salvation of the righteous comes from the LORD; he is their stronghold in time of trouble. The LORD helps them and delivers them" (Psalm 37:39-40). "Those who look to him are radiant; their faces are never covered with shame" (Psalm 34:5).

Do You Know?

The crew of the *Dawn Treader* realizes that they are seeing "what so many people have foolishly wanted to see—the great Sea Serpent." The Bible tells us about a sea creature with great shining eyes, "fearsome teeth" (Job 41:14), and a hide-like armor—impervious to swords, spears, or arrows. "When he rises up, the mighty are terrified; they retreat before his thrashing. . . . He makes the depths churn like a boiling caldron. . . . Behind him he leaves a glistening wake" (Job 41:25, 31-32). Do you know what this creature is called?

(Hint: Read Job 41:1.)

Scriptures on Escaping the Dangers of Temptation and Corruption
2 Timothy 2:23-26   2 Peter 1:2-3   1 Corinthians 10:12-13

9. THE ISLAND OF THE VOICES

My thoughts trouble me and I am distraught at the voice of the enemy. PSALM 55:2-3

Biblical Parallels and Principles

⨝ Caspian and the others courageously determine to face their invisible enemies and fight as best they can. Later Lucy bravely accepts the task the Voices have given her. Ephesians 6:10 urges believers to "be strong in the Lord and in his mighty power." Philippians 1:27-28 says, "Whatever happens, conduct yourselves in a manner worthy of the gospel of Christ . . . stand firm in one spirit, contending as one man for the faith of the gospel without being frightened in any way by those who oppose you." In Isaiah 41:10 God promises, "I will strengthen you and help you; I will uphold you with my righteous right hand."

⨝ Lucy questions whether she should put much stock in the Voices' fear of the magician. After all, they are "not very brave" and, as Edmund points out, "not very clever." In Isaiah 8:12-13 God tells His people not to be influenced by others' superstitions: "Do not call conspiracy everything that these people call conspiracy; do not fear what they fear, and do not dread it. The LORD Almighty . . . is the one you are to fear, he is the one you are to dread."

Do You Know?

Lucy is called on to do what none of the Voices are brave enough to do themselves. The Bible tells us of a time when the men of Israel called on a woman to do what they were afraid to do—lead the army into battle! Do you remember the woman's name?

(Hint: Read Judges 4:4-10.)

Scriptures on Having a Way with Words

Ecclesiastes 9:17   Proverbs 10:19   Proverbs 17:27-28

10. THE MAGICIAN'S BOOK

"Those whom I love I rebuke and discipline." REVELATION 3:19

Biblical Parallels and Principles

❦ Lucy always feels inferior to Susan. She is tempted to say a spell that will make her more beautiful than her sister. Proverbs 31:30 says, "Charm is deceptive, and beauty is fleeting; but a woman who fears the LORD is to be praised." True beauty comes from within. First Peter 3:3-4 describes it as "the unfading beauty of a gentle and quiet spirit, which is of great worth in God's sight."

❦ Lucy is heartbroken by Marjorie's betrayal of her, but Aslan rebukes Lucy for eavesdropping. He tells Lucy that the younger girl did not mean what she said. The Bible reminds us that at one time or another, we have all said things we did not mean. We cannot judge someone else's heart (1 Samuel 16:7; Matthew 7:1). Ecclesiastes 7:21 says, "Do not pay attention to every word people say, or you may hear your servant cursing you— for you know in your heart that many times you yourself have cursed others."

❦ Lucy's spirit is refreshed by "the loveliest story" she ever read, one that Aslan promises to tell her for "years and years." The most wonderful story in all the world is the story of John 3:16: "For God so loved the world that he gave his one and only Son, that whoever believes in him shall not perish but have eternal life." It, too, is a story about a cup (Matthew 26:39) and a sword (Matthew 26:50-54; 10:34) and a tree (Matthew 27:32; Galatians 3:13) and a hill (Matthew 27:33).

❦ Aslan asks Lucy, "Do you think I wouldn't obey my own rules?" In Matthew 5:17-18 Jesus told His disciples, "Do not think that I have come to abolish the Law or the Prophets; I have not come to abolish them but to fulfill them. I tell you the truth, until heaven and earth disappear, not the smallest letter, not the least stroke of a pen, will by any means disappear from the Law until everything is accomplished." In other words, He obeys His own rules.

Do You Know?

When Lucy sees Aslan, her face lights up with the beauty of "that other Lucy" in the picture. According to the Bible, what is it that makes our faces beautiful?

(Hint: Read 2 Corinthians 3:18; 4:6.)

Scriptures on the Invisible God

Romans 1:20   Colossians 1:15-16   1 Timothy 1:17

11. THE DUFFLEPUDS
MADE HAPPY

*Wisdom calls aloud . . . "How long will you simple ones love
your simple ways? . . . If you had responded to my rebuke,
I would have poured out my heart to you and made my thoughts
known to you."* PROVERBS 1:20-23

Biblical Parallels and Principles

ॐ Coriakin longs for the day when the Duffers can be governed by wisdom
instead of "this rough magic." The Scripture tells us that, in a similar
way, God had to give us the Law to teach us right from wrong—and to
show us the sinfulness of our own hearts (Romans 7:7). "The law was put
in charge to lead us to Christ" (Galatians 3:24). God looked forward to
the time when we would be reconciled to Him through Jesus' death on
the cross. Now, God says, "I will put my laws on their hearts, and I will
write them on their minds" (Hebrews 10:16).

ॐ Aslan says, "I call all times soon." Second Peter 3:8 tells us that "With
the Lord a day is like a thousand years, and a thousand years are like a
day."

ॐ The Duffers think that Coriakin is a hard taskmaster, when in reality
everything he requires of them is for their own benefit. The Scripture
says that all of God's commandments are for our benefit (Psalm 19:7-11;
Deuteronomy 30:11, 15-16). He disciplines us for our good (Hebrews
12:10). Yet many people reject God as a heartless dictator. Half of the time
they regard Him with fear and suspicion, the other half with disrespect
and scorn. Describing such people, Jesus said, "Though seeing, they do
not see; though hearing, they do not hear or understand. . . . For this people's heart has become calloused; they hardly hear with their ears, and
they have closed their eyes. Otherwise they might see with their eyes,
hear with their ears, understand with their hearts and turn, and I would
heal them" (Matthew 13:13-15).

Think About It!

Coriakin reminds Lucy that Aslan is not "a tame lion." He is unpredictable; he cannot be controlled or manipulated. Romans 11:34-35 exclaims, "Who has known the mind of the Lord? Or who has been his counselor? Who has ever given to God that God should repay him?" How does the Bible say God's ways are different from ours?

(Hint: Read Isaiah 55:8-9.)

Scriptures on the Wisdom of God

Romans 11:33-36   1 Corinthians 1:20-21, 25-28   Revelation 7:12

12. THE DARK ISLAND

A word was secretly brought to me, my ears caught a whisper of it. Amid disquieting dreams in the night, when deep sleep falls on men, fear and trembling seized me and made all my bones shake.
JOB 4:12-13

Biblical Parallels and Principles

ȵ&#x8; Lucy calls out to Aslan in her distress—and he answers her. Psalm 145:18-19 says, "The LORD is near to all who call on him . . . he hears their cry and saves them." (See also Psalm 34:6; 120:1; 1 John 5:14-15.) Psalm 55:22 says, "Cast your cares on the LORD and he will sustain you; he will never let the righteous fall."

ȵ&#x8; Lucy draws strength from Aslan's words—and from the assurance of his presence. In Isaiah 43:1-2 God says to His people, "Fear not, for I have redeemed you; I have summoned you by name; you are mine. When you pass through the waters I will be with you." Psalm 46:1 tells us, "God is our refuge and strength, an ever-present help in trouble." Jesus told His disciples, "Surely I am with you always, to the very end of the age" (Matthew 28:20).

ȵ&#x8; The albatross (Aslan) rescues the *Dawn Treader*. He leads them from fear and darkness into the light. The Bible tells us that God will do the same for us. Psalm 91:5 promises, "You will not fear the terror of night." "I will turn the darkness into light" (Isaiah 42:16; see also Psalm 18:28; 139:12). Jesus said, "I am the light of the world. Whoever follows me will never walk in darkness, but will have the light of life" (John 8:12). Colossians 1:13 says that God "has rescued us from the dominion of darkness and brought us into the kingdom of the Son he loves"—"the kingdom of light" (v. 12).

⊶⧫⊷

Do You Know?

Aslan appears in the form of an albatross, piercing the darkness with a ray of light. Lucy hears his voice whisper, "Courage, dear heart." The Bible tells of a time when the sky opened, the Spirit of God appeared in the form of a bird, and people heard His voice speaking. Do you remember when this happened?

(Hint: Read Mark 1:10-11.)

Scriptures on Trust and Peace

Psalm 56:3   Isaiah 26:3   John 14:27

13. THE THREE SLEEPERS

They were all sleeping, because the LORD had put them into a deep sleep. 1 SAMUEL 26:12

Biblical Parallels and Principles

Throughout their adventures, Reepicheep is always challenging the others to be bold and brave and to do what they know is right. Time after time they rise to the challenge, inspired by his example. Proverbs 27:17 observes, "As iron sharpens iron, so one man sharpens another." Hebrews 10:24 says, "Let us consider how we may spur one another on to love and good deeds."

The enchantment has been brought on by a violent argument between the three Lords. Proverbs 22:24-25 says, "Do not make friends with a hot-tempered man, do not associate with one easily angered, or you may learn his ways and get yourself ensnared." Proverbs 20:3 tells us, "It is to a man's honor to avoid strife, but every fool is quick to quarrel."

The girl says, "You can't know. You can only believe—or not." As Christians, we are called to live by faith (2 Corinthians 5:7; Galatians 2:20). In His earthly ministry, Jesus often chided His disciples for their lack of faith (Matthew 8:26; 14:31; Luke 9:41). He healed countless others in response to their faith (Matthew 8:1-3, 13; 9:2, 22; 15:28). Sometimes He asked them first if they believed (for example, Matthew 9:28). One man responded, "I do believe; help me overcome my unbelief!" (Mark 9:24).

Caspian "obeyed" Reepicheep's request. Kings and Queens of Narnia are not to be ruthless dictators or demanding tyrants. They have been called to protect and serve their free subjects. (See *The Magician's Nephew*, Chapter Eleven.) Jesus taught His disciples that whoever would be great in the kingdom of God must be a servant of others (Matthew 20:25-28; John 13:3-7). Galatians 5:13 says, "You, my brothers, were called to be free. But do not use your freedom to indulge the sinful nature; rather, serve one another in love." And Ephesians 5:21 tells believers, "Submit to one another out of reverence for Christ."

Think About It!

The Stone Knife is an instrument of torture and death. With it the White Witch killed Aslan. Since his resurrection, it has become a treasured symbol—not only of his sacrifice, but of his victory and triumph. For Christians, there is an instrument of death and torture that is now a symbol of sacrifice and triumph. We hang this symbol in our churches and wear it around our necks. What is it?

(Hint: Read Colossians 2:13-15.)

Scriptures on Sleep That Is Sweet

Psalm 4:8   Psalm 127:1-2   Proverbs 3:21-24

14. THE BEGINNING OF THE END OF THE WORLD

Who is this that appears like the dawn, fair as the moon, bright as the sun, majestic as the stars in procession? SONG OF SONGS 6:10

Biblical Parallels and Principles

❧ Ramandu and his daughter lift up their arms in a kind of worship, singing to welcome—or bring about—the sunrise. Psalm 148:1-3 says, "Praise the LORD from the heavens, praise him in the heights above. Praise him, all his angels, praise him, all his heavenly hosts. Praise him, sun and moon, praise him, all you shining stars." (See also Job 38:7.) Psalm 57:7-9 says, "I will sing and make music. . . . I will awaken the dawn. I will praise you, O Lord, among the nations; I will sing of you among the peoples. For great is your love, reaching to the heavens."

❧ A bird lays a fire-berry—"like a little live coal"—in the Old Man's mouth. Though the purpose is different, the description of the scene is similar to that of Isaiah 6:6-7: "One of the seraphs flew to me with a live coal in his hand. . . . With it he touched my mouth." In 1 Kings 17:2-6 God ordered ravens to feed the prophet Elijah: They "brought him bread and meat in the morning and bread and meat in the evening."

❧ Ramandu is rejuvenated by the fire-berries. He grows younger instead of older. Second Corinthians 4:16-17 describes a similar process that takes place in a believer's spirit: "Though outwardly we are wasting away, yet inwardly we are being renewed day by day."

❧ Caspian shocks the crew by telling them that he is not asking for volunteers: He is issuing an invitation and choosing from those who respond. In the Parable of the Wedding Banquet, Jesus explained that everyone is invited to Heaven, but only those who put their trust in Him will be welcomed in. "Many are invited, but few are chosen" (Matthew 22:14). Some, like Pittencream or the guest without wedding clothes, will lose their chance.

Do You Know?

In Narnia, a star that has fallen to earth is "a star at rest" (like Ramandu) or a star being disciplined (like Coriakin). The Bible tells us about a "star" that fell from Heaven, taking a third of the other "stars" with him. (Unlike Coriakin, these stars cannot repent or be rehabilitated.) Do you know who or what they really are?

(Hint: Read Isaiah 14:12-15; Luke 10:18; Revelation 9:1; 12:3-4, 9.)

Scriptures on Answering the Call

John 7:37-38   Revelation 3:20   Matthew 16:24-27

15. THE WONDERS OF THE LAST SEA

Light is sweet, and it pleases the eye to see the sun. ECCLESIASTES 11:7

Biblical Parallels and Principles

🐾 Despite nearly drowning, Reepicheep can't contain his excitement. The prophecy he received in his infancy is about to come true: They are drawing near to Aslan's country. Proverbs 13:19 says, "A longing fulfilled is sweet to the soul."

🐾 Reepicheep's longing for Aslan's country is like the desire of believers to see Heaven and experience the presence of God. Hebrews 11:13-16 tells us that the heroes of our faith, men and women of old, considered themselves to be aliens and strangers on this earth. "They were longing for a better country—a heavenly one. Therefore God is not ashamed to be called their God, for he has prepared a city for them."

Did You Know?

Narnia is a flat world; so Caspian is shocked to discover that the "fairy-tales" are true: Round worlds (like ours) do exist! For thousands of years scientists believed our world was flat. It was only five hundred years ago that Columbus and other explorers proved that one could sail around it. But long before Columbus or Galileo, long before telescopes and rockets and space probes, the psalmist wrote about the sun traveling its "circuit" (Psalm 19:6). And the prophet Isaiah told us that God "sits enthroned above the circle of the earth" (Isaiah 40:22).

Scriptures on the Light of the Righteous

Psalm 97:11-12   1 Peter 2:9   2 Corinthians 4:6

16. THE VERY END OF THE WORLD

I am a rose of Sharon, a lily of the valleys. SONG OF SONGS 2:1

Biblical Parallels and Principles

⮞ In the brilliant light at the edge of Aslan's country, the children see a tall wave that appears like a wall of "wonderful rainbow colors." Beyond that are lush forests, waterfalls, and mountains. Where the sky meets the earth, it appears like glass. Compare this description to that of the New Jerusalem—the Heavenly City of God—in Revelation 21—22. The city is seen from "a mountain great and high," shining brilliantly with the glory of God (21:10-11). High walls surround the city, "decorated with every kind of precious stone"—a rainbow of colored jewels such as jasper, sapphire, emerald, topaz, and amethyst (21:18-21). "The river of the water of life" flows "from the throne of God . . . as clear as crystal" (22:1-2). There are luscious fruit trees (22:2). The walls, the city itself, and even the streets appear pure as glass (21:18, 21).

⮞ Reepicheep tries to be sad about saying good-bye, but he is too excited! The Bible tells us, "No eye has seen, no ear has heard, no mind has conceived what God has prepared for those who love him" (1 Corinthians 2:9).

⮞ The Lamb welcomes the children ashore: "Come and have breakfast." After His resurrection, Jesus appeared to His disciples by the Sea of Galilee. "Early in the morning, Jesus stood on the shore, but the disciples did not realize that it was Jesus. . . . Jesus said to them, 'Come and have breakfast'" (John 21:4, 12). The disciples suddenly recognized Him. He served them a breakfast of bread and fish. And after they had finished eating, Jesus shared with them words of instruction and encouragement.

⮞ The Lamb becomes a Lion, and the children realize it is Aslan himself. The Bible tells us that Jesus is the Lion of Judah (Revelation 5:5). He is also "the Lamb of God, who takes away the sin of the world" (John 1:29; see also Isaiah 53:7; 1 Peter 1:19; Revelation 5:6-14; 7:10, 17; 19:7).

⮞ Aslan says that the way to his country from our world lies across a river: "But do not fear that, for I am the great Bridge Builder." In hymns, poems, and stories, Christians have often referred to death as "crossing the river," because in the Old Testament the Israelites had to cross the River Jordan to get to the Promised Land (Joshua 1:2). We all have to die one day, and death is the way we cross from this world to the next—to Heaven. Scripture says that we have been separated from God by our sin

(Isaiah 59:2; Romans 3:23). It comes between us and God like a great gulf or chasm (Luke 16:26). But by dying in our place and paying the penalty for our sin, Jesus makes it possible for us to be reconciled to God (2 Corinthians 5:17-19). Jesus laid down His life for us (1 John 3:16), becoming—as C.S. Lewis said—our great "Bridge Builder."

Lucy and Edmund must learn to know Aslan by his other name in our world. Years ago, after reading this passage in *Dawn Treader*, a little girl named Hila wrote to C.S. Lewis, asking him to tell her Aslan's other name. Lewis responded, "Well, I want you to guess. Has there ever been anyone in this world who 1) arrived at the same time as Father Christmas, 2) Said he was the son of the Great Emperor, 3) Gave himself up for someone else's fault to be jeered at and killed by wicked people, 4) Came to life again, 5) Is sometimes spoken of as a lamb. Don't you really know His name in this world? Think it over and let me know your answer." Aslan's other name is "the name above all names"—Jesus (Philippians 2:9-11).

Do You Know?

Like Lucy, King Caspian has a heart that is sensitive to spiritual things. He longs for a deeper experience. Though it is not wrong for Caspian to *want* to journey to Aslan's country, he cannot go. The Bible tells us that King David had a heart sensitive to spiritual things. He wanted to do something very special for God, and though the desire itself wasn't wrong, God said, "No." Do you remember what it was David wanted to do?

(Hint: Read 1 Kings 8:17-19.)

Scriptures on Having a Heart for God
Mark 12:30   Psalm 84:1-2   Psalm 86:11

THE
SILVER
CHAIR

Introduction to

The Silver Chair

And the lesson of it all is . . . that those Northern Witches always mean the same thing, but in every age they have a different plan for getting it. THE SILVER CHAIR

As *The Silver Chair* begins, Eustace and his classmate, Jill, are trying to escape the school bullies. Slipping through a door, they suddenly find themselves in Aslan's country. He has summoned them to embark on an important quest: The children must find and rescue Prince Rilian, the son of King Caspian the Tenth, who disappeared from Narnia more than ten years earlier. He was last seen in the company of a lovely woman whom wise old Narnians fear to be an enchantress. The children will be guided by a dour Marsh-wiggle named Puddleglum. Their quest will take them through Narnia into the Wild Wastelands of the North and under the ancient ruins of a giant city. There they will discover that the Prince's kidnapping is part of an elaborate plot devised by the enchantress with one goal in mind: to conquer and enslave the people of Narnia once again.

The Silver Chair explores many spiritual themes that are especially relevant to Christians today—not the least of which is the importance of staying on guard, being aware of and alert to the enemy's schemes. "Satan himself masquerades as an angel of light . . . his servants masquerade as servants of righteousness" (2 Corinthians 11:14-15). Prince Rilian was deceived by the beauty of the enchantress. The children mistake her for a friend. Only Puddleglum remains suspicious.

Disaster threatens when the children listen to the witch's lies and allow themselves to be distracted from following Aslan's commands. Aslan had given them four signs to watch for. He warned Jill, "Remember, remember, remember the signs." He instructed her to repeat them to herself night and day. "These commandments that I give to you today are to be upon your hearts. Impress them on your children. Talk about them when you sit at home and when you walk along the road, when you lie down and when you get up. Tie them as symbols on your hands and bind them on your foreheads. Write them on the doorframes of your houses and on your gates" (Deuteronomy 6:6-9).

Neglecting the signs makes the children vulnerable to the witch's deception. When they manage to escape a trap she has set for them, the witch tries a more subtle approach. She questions their faith in Aslan, confuses their thoughts, and ridicules their attempts to explain what they believe. Regardless of her enchanting words, Puddleglum is steadfast and resolute. He may not be able to win a debate with one so skilled at twisting the truth, but he knows what he believes, and to that he will be true. "I know whom I have believed, and am persuaded that he is able to keep that which I have committed unto him against that day" (2 Timothy 1:12, KJV). Puddleglum's unshakable faith saves the day. "The weapons we fight with are not the weapons of the world. On the contrary, they have divine power to demolish strongholds. We demolish arguments and every pretension that sets itself up against the knowledge of God, and we take captive every thought to make it obedient to Christ" (2 Corinthians 10:4-5).

The children discover that in spite of their own shortcomings—their mistakes and failures all along the way—Aslan's purposes prevail. With Aslan's help, they get back on track, find the Prince, and set him free from his bondage to the witch's Silver Chair. "For it is God who works in you to will and to act according to his good purpose" (Philippians 2:13). His grace is sufficient for us—His power is made perfect in our weakness (2 Corinthians 12:9).

The story of Jill and Eustace's adventures also includes powerful illustrations of the following truths: "Whoever drinks of the water I [Jesus] give him will never thirst. Indeed, the water I give him will become in him a spring of water welling up to eternal life" (John 4:13-14). "The blood of Jesus . . . cleanses us from all sin" (1 John 1:7, ESV). "Our light and momentary troubles are achieving for us an eternal glory that far outweighs them all" (2 Corinthians 4:17).

These lessons are just a few of the spiritual treasures you will discover as you journey with Jill and Eustace to rescue Prince Rilian from *The Silver Chair*.

1. BEHIND THE GYM

Send forth your light and your truth, let them guide me; let them bring me to your holy mountain, to the place where you dwell.

PSALM 43:3

Biblical Parallels and Principles

꙳ Eustace doesn't think Aslan would like it if they try to contact him by reciting charms and spells. And anyway, their wish is *not* Aslan's command. They can't make him respond—they can only ask. In Deuteronomy 18:10-12 God specifically forbids any and every kind of occult activity, including the casting of spells. "Anyone who does these things is detestable to the LORD." And Acts 17:24-25 reminds us that "the God who made the world and everything in it is the Lord of heaven and earth . . . he himself gives all men life and breath and everything else." He does not answer to us—we answer to Him!

꙳ Eustace begins to call out to Aslan for help. He is praying as best he can. Psalm 145:18-19 says, "The LORD is near to all who call on him, to all who call on him in truth. He fulfills the desires of those who fear him; he hears their cry and saves them."

Do You Know?

Jill has noticed the change in Eustace. Since his adventures in Narnia (in *The Voyage of the Dawn Treader*), he has become a completely different person. Instead of supporting the school bullies, he stands up to them. The Bible tells us about someone who had an experience that changed him completely. After killing Christians, he became one. Do you remember his name?

(Hint: Read Acts 9:1-19.)

Scriptures on a Changed Life

2 Corinthians 5:17   Ephesians 4:22-24   Romans 12:1-2

2. JILL IS GIVEN A TASK

Whoever is thirsty, let him come; and whoever wishes, let him take the free gift of the water of life. REVELATION 22:17

Biblical Parallels and Principles

∾ Jill says she is *dying* of thirst. "As the deer pants for streams of water, so my soul pants for you, O God. My soul thirsts for God, for the living God. . . . My tears have been my food day and night" (Psalm 42:1-3). The psalmist cried, "O God you are my God, earnestly I seek you; my soul thirsts for you, my body longs for you, in a dry and weary land where there is no water" (Psalm 63:1).

∾ Aslan invites Jill to drink from the stream. Jesus said, "If anyone is thirsty, let him come to me and drink. Whoever believes in me, as the Scripture has said, streams of living water will flow from within him" (John 7:37; see also John 4:4-14).

∾ Jill is afraid of Aslan; she would rather find another stream. But Aslan says there is no other stream. The Bible tells us that Jesus is the only source of living water—the "spring of water welling up to eternal life" (John 4:13-14). He said, "I am the way and the truth and the life. No one comes to the Father except through me" (John 14:6).

∾ Jill can't bear to look into Aslan's eyes. His gaze overwhelms her; she feels guilty and ashamed. The Gospel of Luke tells us that when Peter denied Jesus for the third time, a rooster crowed. "The Lord turned and looked straight at Peter . . . he [Peter] went outside and wept bitterly" (Luke 22:61-62).

∾ Jill knows that what she has done is wrong. Aslan commends her for being honest and forthright. As for her sin, he says, "Do so no more." These words are nearly identical to those of Jesus in John 8:11. To the woman caught in adultery, Jesus said that He did not condemn her: "Go, and sin no more" (KJV).

∾ Aslan tells Jill to speak her thoughts; he knows them already. Hebrews 4:13 reminds us, "Nothing in all creation is hidden from God's sight. Everything is uncovered and laid bare before the eyes of him to whom we must give account."

∾ The Lion explains, "You would not have called to me unless I had been calling to you." Jesus told His disciples, "You did not choose me, but I chose you" (John 15:16). The Scripture makes it clear that God is the One who takes the initiative—He is the One who calls and reaches out to us (Romans 3:11; 5:8; Isaiah 1:18; 45:22; Revelation 3:20). He is also the One who enables us to respond to His call. "For it is God who works in you to will and to act according to his good purpose" (Philippians 2:13). Aslan tells Jill, "Remember, remember, remember the signs." He instructs her to repeat them to herself day and night. In Deuteronomy 6:6-9 God says, "These commandments that I give to you today are to be upon your hearts. Impress them on your children. Talk about them when you sit at home and when you walk along the road, when you lie down and when you get up. Tie them as symbols on your hands and bind them on your foreheads. Write them on the doorframes of your houses and on your gates."

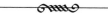

Think About It!

Aslan warns Jill that the signs will not look as she expects them to look. "That is why it is so important to know them by heart and pay no attention to appearances." The Old Testament contains hundreds of signs—prophecies—about the coming of the Messiah. When Jesus came, He fulfilled every one of them. But somehow people missed the signs. They didn't look the way they expected them to. "He was in the world, and though the world was made through him, the world did not recognize him. He came to that which was his own, but his own did not receive him" (John 1:10-11). As Christians, this is something for us to think about—especially as we study the "signs" in anticipation of His Second Coming.

Scriptures on Remembering God's Commands

Psalm 119:9-13   Psalm 119:97-102   Proverbs 4:4-5

3. THE SAILING OF THE KING

Love is patient, love is kind. It does not envy, it does not boast, it is not proud. It is not rude, it is not self-seeking, it is not easily angered, it keeps no record of wrongs. 1 CORINTHIANS 13:4-5

Biblical Parallels and Principles

❧ Eustace and Jill cannot stop bickering and blaming each other for the mess they are in. Proverbs 17:14 observes, "Starting a quarrel is like breaching a dam; so drop the matter before a dispute breaks out." Ephesians 4:26-27, 31-32 tells us: "Do not let the sun go down while you are still angry, and do not give the devil a foothold. . . . Get rid of all bitterness, rage and anger. . . . Be kind and compassionate to one another, forgiving each other, just as in Christ God forgave you."

❧ Jill's showing off on the mountain and Eustace's carrying a grudge causes them to muff the first sign. The Scripture warns us that sin can have terrible consequences (James 1:14-15; Deuteronomy 30:15-18). That is why it is so important to obey God's Word. "Do not let this Book of the Law depart from your mouth; meditate on it day and night, so that you may be careful to do everything written in it. Then you will be prosperous and successful" (Joshua 1:8).

Do You Know?

When Trumpkin finally realizes that Aslan has sent the strangers, he welcomes them gladly. The Bible tells us to practice hospitality and to welcome the strangers among us. Do you know why?

(Hint: Read Hebrews 13:2.)

Scriptures on Forgiving One Another

Matthew 6:14-15   Matthew 18:21-22   Colossians 3:13

4. A PARLIAMENT OF OWLS

Hear my prayer, O LORD; let my cry for help come to you. Do not hide your face from me when I am in distress. . . . I am like . . . an owl among the ruins. I lie awake; I have become like a bird alone on a roof. PSALM 102:1-2, 6-7

Biblical Parallels and Principles

⅋ In the King's absence, Trumpkin will stick to the rules—even when there's a very good reason to make an exception. Caspian's rule was never meant to keep the children from obeying Aslan! Jesus pointed out that some people are experts at following the letter of the Law, but they completely miss or violate its spirit. (See Matthew 12:1-12; Mark 7:1-13.) Galatians 4:18 says, "It is fine to be zealous, provided the purpose is good."

⅋ The Narnians believe that the serpent and the green lady are one and the same—and that she is of the same ilk as the White Witch. The years come and go, names and faces change, but the enemy is the same and has the same purpose. The Bible tells us that Satan "was a murderer from the beginning" (John 8:44). He was cast out of Heaven before time began. "The great dragon was hurled down—that ancient serpent called the devil, or Satan, who leads the whole world astray" (Revelation 12:9). When he couldn't prevent Christ's atonement for mankind, he went off to make war against all of "those who obey God's commandments and hold to the testimony of Jesus" (Revelation 12:17). He "masquerades as an angel of light" (2 Corinthians 11:14). But always his purpose is evil. He comes to "steal and kill and destroy" (John 10:10).

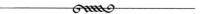

Do You Know?

Though his intentions were good, Drinian discovered that keeping the Prince's secret was a terrible mistake. The Bible says some secrets should be kept (Proverbs 11:13; Matthew 18:15). But when should we speak up? (Hint: Read Proverbs 24:11-12; 27:5; and Galatians 6:1.)

Scriptures on Seeking God's Face in a Time of Trouble

1 Chronicles 16:11   Psalm 27:7-8   2 Chronicles 7:14

5. PUDDLEGLUM

Be strong and take heart, all you who hope in the Lord.

PSALM 31:24

Biblical Parallels and Principles

❧ Puddleglum always expects the worst. The children find his perspective terribly discouraging; yet Puddleglum himself is not discouraged. The dangers and disasters he anticipates are very real; some of them will, in fact, come to pass. Puddleglum expects them and is therefore prepared to face them. Jesus warned His disciples to count the cost of following Him (Luke 14:25-33). They needed to be prepared. "Any of you who does not give up everything he has cannot be my disciple" (v. 33; see also John 15:18-21; Matthew 10:16-22).

❧ Although he is frightened by Puddleglum's dire predictions, Eustace refuses to believe that their quest is hopeless—or Aslan would never have sent them. Joshua 1:9 says, "Be strong and courageous. Do not be terrified; do not be discouraged, for the LORD your God will be with you wherever you go." The psalmist said, "As for me, I will always have hope" (Psalm 71:14). The apostle Paul explained, "We have put our hope in the living God, who is the Savior of all men" (1 Timothy 4:10). "On him we have set our hope that he will continue to deliver us" (2 Corinthians 1:10).

Can That Be Right?
Puddleglum's friends say he doesn't take life seriously enough! But does he really need to be *more* "glum"? What does the Bible say our outlook should be?

(Hint: Read Philippians 4:4-9.)

Scriptures on Quarreling
Proverbs 20:3   Philippians 2:14   2 Timothy 2:23-24

6. THE WILD WASTE LANDS OF THE NORTH

*We want each of you to show this same diligence to the very end,
in order to make your hope sure. We do not want you to become
lazy.* HEBREWS 6:11-12

Biblical Parallels and Principles

❧ Whether dealing with giants, beautiful ladies, or mysterious knights,
Puddleglum remains alert and suspicious—always on guard. Proverbs
14:15 says, "A simple man believes anything, but a prudent man gives
thought to his steps." Proverbs 12:26 observes, "A righteous man is cautious in friendship." And Ephesians 5:15-16 tells believers, "Be very careful, then, how you live—not as unwise, but as wise . . . because the days
are evil."

❧ Puddleglum interrupts Jill and prevents her from revealing their quest.
"A prudent man keeps his knowledge to himself" (Proverbs 12:23).
Proverbs 10:19 adds, "He who holds his tongue is wise." And Proverbs
21:23 observes, "He who guards his mouth and his tongue keeps himself
from calamity." That's why the psalmist prayed, "Set a guard over my
mouth, O LORD; keep watch over the door of my lips" (Psalm 141:3).

❧ Jill has given up the bothersome task of repeating the signs. She is in danger of forgetting them altogether. Scripture urges us to remember God's
commandments always. Psalm 119:16, 93, 109 says: "I delight in your
decrees, I will not neglect your word. . . . I will never forget your precepts,
for by them you have preserved my life. . . . I will not forget your law."

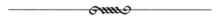

Do You Know?

Eustace and Jill find the Lady of the Green Kirtle beautiful, but Puddleglum
is wary. How does the Bible say Satan and his servants disguise themselves?

(Hint: Read 2 Corinthians 11:14-15.)

Scriptures on Staying Alert

1 Peter 5:8   1 Corinthians 16:13   Ephesians 6:10-13

7. THE HILL OF THE STRANGE TRENCHES

Give careful thought to your ways. HAGGAI 1:5

Biblical Parallels and Principles

As they stumble through the trenches, Puddleglum notices something. He wants to stop and look around to see where they are; he asks Jill to repeat the signs. But Jill and Eustace refuse. Their thoughts are bent on reaching Harfang and its hot baths and cozy beds. The Scripture warns believers that the enemy seeks to distract us from the truth. Hebrews 2:1 says, "We must pay more careful attention, therefore, to what we have heard, so that we do not drift away."

When he has finished his drink, Puddleglum grows disoriented, and his speech becomes garbled. Proverbs 23:20, 33 warns that alcohol can have a powerful effect on a person: "Do not join those who drink too much wine. . . . Your eyes will see strange sights and your mind imagine confusing things."

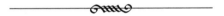

Do You Know?

Eustace and Jill are weary and worn-out. They have almost given up their quest. All that they focus on is getting relief from their temporary troubles. What does the Bible tell us to fix our eyes on?

(Hint: Read 2 Corinthians 4:16-18.)

Scriptures on Paying Attention

Proverbs 4:20-22   Isaiah 48:17-18   Proverbs 16:20

8. THE HOUSE OF HARFANG

Why are you downcast, O my soul? Why so disturbed within me? Put your hope in God, for I will yet praise him, my Savior and my God. PSALM 42:11

Biblical Parallels and Principles

Jill doesn't like the way the giants lick their lips, smile at each other, and laugh. Proverbs 6:12-14 says that "a scoundrel and villain . . . goes about with a corrupt mouth . . . winks with his eye, signals with his feet and motions with his fingers . . . [he] plots evil with deceit in his heart."

Jill and Eustace realize that they have made a serious mistake, overlooking the ancient ruins. They have missed three of the four signs. "This is what the LORD says—your Redeemer, the Holy One of Israel: 'I am the LORD your God, who teaches you what is best for you, who directs you in the way you should go. If only you had paid attention to my commands . . .'" (Isaiah 48:17-18).

Puddleglum says that Aslan's instructions always work. Psalm 19:7-11 tells us that God's commandments are perfect and trustworthy and sure. In Isaiah 55:11 God says, "My word . . . will not return to me empty, but will accomplish what I desire and achieve the purpose for which I sent it." (See also Psalm 119; 2 Timothy 3:16-17.) God promises His people, "Along unfamiliar paths I will guide them; I will turn the darkness into light before them and make the rough places smooth" (Isaiah 42:16).

Jill and the others determine to do their best to make things right. It may not be too late. Second Corinthians 7:10 says, "Godly sorrow brings repentance that leads to salvation." In Revelation 3:19 God says, "Those whom I love I rebuke and discipline." Acts 3:19 urges, "Repent, then, and turn to God so that your sins may be wiped out, that times of refreshing may come from the Lord."

Do You Know?

Jill, Eustace, and Puddleglum plan to act silly and mindless in order to allay the giants' suspicions while they plan their escape. Someone in the Bible pretended to be out of his mind in order to escape his enemies. Do you know who?

(Hint: Read 1 Samuel 21:10-15.)

Scriptures on Dealing with Dangerous People

Matthew 10:16   Ephesians 5:15-17   Colossians 2:8

9. HOW THEY DISCOVERED SOMETHING WORTH KNOWING

Through knowledge the righteous escape. PROVERBS 11:9

Biblical Parallels and Principles

In his horror over eating a Talking stag, Puddleglum exclaims that they have incurred the wrath of Aslan and are probably "under a curse." God does say that He will curse those who are wicked and rebellious. But to His servants, He is merciful: "slow to anger, abounding in love. . . . As a father has compassion on his children, so the LORD has compassion on those who fear him; for he knows how we are formed, he remembers that we are dust" (Psalm 103:8, 13-14).

Puddleglum was right all along. The Lady of the Green Kirtle has sent them right into a trap. Second Peter 2:18 says of the wicked, "By appealing to the lustful desires of sinful human nature, they entice people." Psalm 5:9 warns, "Not a word from their mouth can be trusted; their heart is filled with destruction. Their throat is an open grave; with their tongue they speak deceit."

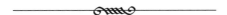

Do You Know?

The hunting party returns in time to give chase to Puddleglum and the children. What does the Bible say wicked men hunt? And what will hunt *them*?

(Hint: Read Psalm 10:2 and Psalm 140:11b.)

Scriptures on Acquiring Knowledge

Proverbs 2:1-12   Proverbs 23:12   James 1:5

10. TRAVELS WITHOUT THE SUN

*We look for light, but all is darkness; for brightness, but we walk
in deep shadows.* ISAIAH 59:9B

Biblical Parallels and Principles

🐸 Though Puddleglum and the children know otherwise, the Prince is convinced that the Queen of the Underland is fair and virtuous. Second
Corinthians 11:14-15 says, "Satan himself masquerades as an angel of
light . . . his servants masquerade as servants of righteousness." Jesus said,
"They come to you in sheep's clothing, but inwardly they are ferocious
wolves. By their fruit you will recognize them" (Matthew 7:15-16).

🐸 Puddleglum insists that "there are no accidents": "Our guide is Aslan; and
he was there when the giant King caused the letters to be cut, and he knew
already all things that would come of them, including *this*." The Bible tells
us that even before Adam and Eve fell, God had planned how to rescue
us from sin's power. Jesus was there from the very beginning. Revelation
13:8 calls Him "the Lamb that was slain from the creation of the world"
(compare John 1:1-3). Speaking of God's omniscience, the psalmist
observed, "You knit me together in my mother's womb. . . . All the days
ordained for me were written in your book before one of them came to
be" (Psalm 139:13, 16). Proverbs 19:21 reminds us of God's sovereignty:
"Many are the plans of a man's heart, but it is the LORD's purpose that
prevails."

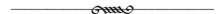

Do You Know?

The Warden tells Puddleglum and the children that the enormous man
sleeping in the cavern is Father Time: "They say he will wake at the end of
the world." And so apparently will the strange beasts on the turf. The Bible
says that at the end of the world certain people will rise from the Deep
Realm. Do you know who?

   (Hint: Read 1 Thessalonians 4:16-17 and 1 Corinthians 15:51-52.)

Scriptures on the Deepest, Darkest Depths

Psalm 139:7-12   Lamentations 3:55   Micah 7:19

11. IN THE DARK CASTLE

He [the Lord] will bring to light what is hidden in darkness.

1 CORINTHIANS 4:5

Biblical Parallels and Principles

❧ The Knight (who is the Prince) begs Puddleglum and the children to set him free, crying, "By the great Lion, by Aslan himself, I charge you—" Philippians 2:9-11 tells us that God has given Jesus "the name that is above every name." His name is powerful—it brings life and healing (John 20:31; Acts 3:16). Jesus Himself promised that He would do whatever we ask in His name (John 14:14; 15:16).

❧ Puddleglum insists that they obey Aslan's command, even though they fear the consequences. Jesus said, "If you love me, you will obey what I command" (John 14:15). He promised that if we obey, He will live in us and through us. He will love us and be with us always. He will give us His peace (John 14:15-27). "And we know that in all things God works for the good of those who love him, who have been called according to his purpose" (Romans 8:28). Proverbs 16:20 says, "Blessed is he who trusts in the LORD."

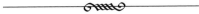

Do You Know?

Puddleglum and the children are confused—they don't know whether or not to believe the Prince. Should they set him free? What does the Bible say believers should do when they truly need guidance?

(Hint: Read Psalm 91:14-15 and James 1:5.)

Scriptures on Setting the Captives Free

Proverbs 24:11-12   Isaiah 61:1   Ezekiel 13:20

12. THE QUEEN OF UNDERLAND

You are all sons of the light and sons of the day. We do not belong to the night or to the darkness. 1 THESSALONIANS 5:5

Biblical Parallels and Principles

The Witch sounds sweet and lovely. Like the evil woman described in Proverbs 5:3, her lips "drip honey, and her speech is smoother than oil." With persuasive words, she leads them astray (Proverbs 7:21). "Many are the victims she has brought down; her slain are a mighty throng" (v. 26). Romans 16:18 observes that this is how the wicked operate: "By smooth talk and flattery they deceive the minds of naive people." Of his enemies, the psalmist said, "All day long they twist my words" (Psalm 56:5). Satan uses the same strategy to confuse believers today.

Though it takes a tremendous effort, Puddleglum resists the enchantment. He refuses to believe the Witch's lies; he stubbornly clings to what he knows is true. In this, he serves as a wonderful example for believers who are under spiritual attack today. The apostle Paul said, "I know whom I have believed, and am persuaded that he is able to keep that which I have committed unto him . . . " (2 Timothy 1:12, KJV; see also John 8:31-32). Ephesians 6:14-16 tells us, "Stand firm then, with the belt of truth buckled around your waist . . . take up the shield of faith, with which you can extinguish all the flaming arrows of the evil one." Second Corinthians 10:4-5 explains, "The weapons we fight with are not the weapons of the world. On the contrary, they have divine power to demolish strongholds. We demolish arguments and every pretension that sets itself up against the knowledge of God, and we take captive every thought to make it obedient to Christ."

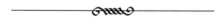

Do You Know?

The Witch says that Aslan and Narnia are make-believe, children's stories. How did Jesus' disciples respond to those who said the same thing about the Gospel?

(Hint: Read Galatians 1:11-12 and 2 Peter 1:16-19.)

Scriptures on Holding Fast to the Truth

Proverbs 4:1-5, 13, 20-23   Philippians 4:8-9   Ephesians 6:10-18

13. UNDERLAND WITHOUT THE QUEEN

I am against your magic charms. . . . I will set free the people
that you ensnare. . . . I will . . . save my people from your hands,
and they will no longer fall prey to your power. EZEKIEL 13:20-21

Biblical Parallels and Principles

Rilian says, "Aslan will be our good Lord, whether he means us to live or die. And all's one, for that." The apostle Paul said, "If we live, we live to the Lord; and if we die, we die to the Lord. So, whether we live or die, we belong to the Lord" (Romans 14:8). "For to me, to live is Christ and to die is gain" (Philippians 1:21). "So we make it our goal to please him, whether we are at home in the body or away from it" (2 Corinthians 5:9).

Rilian tells Jill that if they all die fighting around her, "you must commend yourself to the Lion." The apostle Paul used a similar phrase to refer to putting oneself or one's loved ones into God's hands. (The King James Version uses the word "commend"; modern translations use the word "commit" or "entrust.") For example, see Acts 14:23, 20:32, and 2 Timothy 1:12-14. As Jesus died on the cross, He cried out, "Father, into your hands I commit [commend] my spirit" (Luke 23:46).

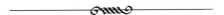

Do You Know?

Rilian, Puddleglum, and the children make their escape through a world apparently rocked by earthquakes, fire, and floods. In the Scriptures, God told His people that they would experience similar circumstances, but that they should not be afraid. Why not?

(Hint: Read Isaiah 43:1-2, 5-7.)

Scriptures on Trusting God Whether We Live or Die

Daniel 3:16-18   2 Corinthians 5:1-10   Philippians 1:19-26

14. THE BOTTOM OF THE WORLD

. . . say to the captives, "Come out," and to those in darkness, "Be free." ISAIAH 49:9

Biblical Parallels and Principles

❦ Fire, floods, earthquakes . . . the travelers realize that what they are witnessing is the deliverance of the Underland. It has suddenly been set free from the dominion of the Witch. The Bible tells us that our world is in bondage—under the curse of sin. It longs to be set free. "We know that the whole creation has been groaning as in the pains of childbirth right up to the present time" (Romans 8:22). And "the creation waits in eager expectation for the sons of God to be revealed . . . in hope that creation itself will be liberated from its bondage to decay and brought into the glorious freedom of the children of God" (Romans 8:19-21).

❦ Rilian repeats his admonition: "Whether we live or die Aslan will be our good Lord." The apostle Paul said, "If we live, we live to the Lord; and if we die, we die to the Lord. So, whether we live or die, we belong to the Lord" (Romans 14:8). "For to me, to live is Christ and to die is gain" (Philippians 1:21). "Therefore we will not fear, though the earth give way and the mountains fall into the heart of the sea. . . . The LORD Almighty is with us" (Psalm 46:2, 7).

Do You Know?

By killing the Witch, Rilian and the others find that they have destroyed her power and have broken all kinds of enchantments with which she held the Underland captive. According to the Bible, Jesus came to our world to destroy certain things. Do you know what things?

(Hint: Read 1 John 3:8 and Revelation 22:3.)

Scriptures on Deliverance

2 Samuel 22:2-3   Psalm 32:6-7   2 Corinthians 1:9-10

15. THE DISAPPEARANCE OF JILL

For he has rescued us from the dominion of darkness and brought us into the kingdom of the Son he loves. COLOSSIANS 1:13

Biblical Parallels and Principles

When Jill sees the joyful reunion between Rilian and his people, she reflects that "their quest had been worth all the pains it cost." The Bible says that one day believers will have the same perspective on their own "quest"—their journey through the trials and tribulations of this life. The apostle Paul said, "I consider that our present sufferings are not worth comparing to the glory that will be revealed in us" (Romans 8:18). "Therefore, we do not lose heart. . . . For our light and momentary troubles are achieving for us an eternal glory that far outweighs them all. So we fix our eyes not on what is seen, but what is unseen. For what is seen is temporary, but what is unseen is eternal" (2 Corinthians 4:16-18).

The Narnians conclude that "those Northern Witches always mean the same thing, but in every age they have a different plan for getting it." The Bible tells us the same is true of Satan. He "was a murderer from the beginning" (John 8:44). He "masquerades as an angel of light" (2 Corinthians 11:14). But always, his purpose is evil. He comes to "steal and kill and destroy" (John 10:10). The apostle Paul instructed believers to take care, so that Satan might not outwit them: "For we are not unaware of his schemes" (2 Corinthians 2:11).

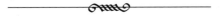

Do You Know?

For many years the Narnian creatures have looked—and longed—for the return of Prince Rilian. But when Jill tells them he has come, they don't believe her. The Bible tells us about a group of people who were praying for the miraculous return of a friend and didn't believe it when God answered their prayers! Do you remember who they prayed for?

(Hint: Read Acts 12:1-16.)

Scriptures on Dancing with Joy

Exodus 15:1-21   Jeremiah 31:13   Psalm 30:11-12

16. THE HEALING OF HARMS

O LORD, the king rejoices in your strength. How great is his joy in the victories you give! You have granted him the desire of his heart and have not withheld the request of his lips. PSALM 21:1-2

Biblical Parallels and Principles

৺ Aslan tells Eustace and Jill that he will "not always be scolding." Psalm 103:8-12 explains, "The LORD is compassionate and gracious, slow to anger, abounding in love. He will not always accuse, nor will he harbor his anger forever; he does not treat us as our sins deserve or repay us according to our iniquities. For as high as the heavens are above the earth, so great is his love for those who fear him; as far as the east is from the west, so far has he removed our transgressions from us."

৺ In spite of their blunders, Aslan commends the children: "You have done the work for which I sent you into Narnia." Jesus used similar language as He described the fulfillment of God's eternal plans. He told His disciples, "We must do the work of him who sent me" (John 9:4). God Himself works in us "to will and to act according to his good purpose" (Philippians 2:13). Though we make mistakes at times—and even fail—God will accomplish what He has ordained. His grace is sufficient for us; His power is made perfect in our weakness (2 Corinthians 12:9-10).

৺ The children mourn the death of King Caspian. "Even the Lion wept: great Lion-tears." Compare this scene to John 11:1-44. Jesus arrived at the tomb of His friend, Lazarus. He was "deeply moved in spirit" (v. 33) as He saw the grief of Lazarus' family, and He grieved with them. "Jesus wept" (v. 35). Then He raised Lazarus from the dead.

৺ Aslan directs Eustace to drive a thorn into his paw. One drop of Aslan's blood washes over Caspian and raises him from death to eternal life in Aslan's country. The Bible tells us that "without the shedding of blood there is no forgiveness" (Hebrews 9:22). Jesus was "pierced for our transgressions, he was crushed for our iniquities; the punishment that brought us peace was upon him, and by his wounds we are healed" (Isaiah 53:5). "For God was pleased to have all his fullness dwell in him, and through him to reconcile to himself all things . . . by making peace through his blood, shed on the cross" (Colossians 1:19-20). "And the blood of Jesus . . . cleanses us from all sin" (1 John 1:7, ESV).

✣ Aslan says of Caspian, "He has died. Most people have, you know. Even I have." Romans 14:9 tells us, "For this very reason, Christ died and returned to life so that he might be the Lord of both the dead and the living." (See also Revelation 1:18.)

✣ Aslan breathes on Jill and Eustace as if to give them power and strength for the task ahead. In John 20:21-22, Jesus breathed on His disciples and told them to receive the Holy Spirit, who would empower them for the tasks ahead of them (also see Acts 1:8).

✣ Aslan gives Caspian, Jill, and Eustace the task of punishing the school bullies for their cruelty. Many times in the Scriptures (especially in the Old Testament), God gave His people the responsibility of carrying out His vengeance against the evil nations around them. (See Numbers 31:3; Deuteronomy 9:1-4; 1 Samuel 15:3.) Proverbs 11:8 says, "A righteous man is rescued from trouble, and it comes on the wicked instead."

Sound Familiar?

Aslan says that he will not reveal himself fully to the gang at Experiment House. They will only see his back. The Bible tells us about someone who wanted to see God's face. God said that the sight would overpower the man and kill him. Instead, He said, He would let the man see His back. Do you remember the man's name?

(Hint: Read Exodus 33:18-23.)

Scriptures on the Blood of Jesus
Ephesians 1:3-8   1 Peter 1:18-21   Revelation 1:5-6; 5:9

THE
LAST
BATTLE

Introduction to

The Last Battle

In the last days of Narnia, far up to the west beyond Lantern Waste and close behind the waterfall, there lived an Ape.

THE LAST BATTLE

When Shift the Ape stumbles upon a lion skin, a plot is born that will spell ruin for Narnia. Shift convinces his donkey friend Puzzle to wear the lion skin and pretend to be Aslan. In Aslan's name, Shift will orchestrate the complete destruction of all that is good and right and true. He will conspire with Narnia's archenemies, the Calormenes, to plunder the forests and rivers, conquer the castle of Cair Paravel, and sell all the creatures into slavery. Jesus warned, "Watch out that no one deceives you. Many will come in my name, claiming, 'I am he,' and will deceive many" (Mark 13:5-6).

Like most Narnians, King Tirian is at first perplexed. Could Aslan really have come secretly to Narnia, and could he be as cruel and unjust as those who purport to be acting in his name? "He's not a tame lion." But when Shift claims that Aslan and the Calormene god Tash are one and the same, Tirian knows it must be a deception. "Any such person is the deceiver and the antichrist" (2 John 7). Tirian asks "how the terrible god Tash who fed on the blood of his people could possibly be the same as the good Lion by whose blood all Narnia was saved."

Unfortunately, many of his subjects are deceived. In fear of "Tashlan's" wrath, they blindly obey Shift's commands. Tirian cries out to the true Aslan to return to Narnia again—or at least to send some of those "children from another world" who always seemed to come when things were at their worst. To the King's amazement, Jill and Eustace suddenly appear before him—ready to rescue him and all of Narnia. But this time Narnia cannot be rescued. Its days are numbered.

King Tirian, Jewel the Unicorn, the children, and a few others try to fend off the darkness. They know from the start that it is a losing battle, but they will fight to their last breath for truth and righteousness. "Be faithful, even to the point of death, and I [Jesus] will give you the crown of life" (Revelation 2:10).

One by one, they are sent through the Stable Door to face the executioner—only to find not death, but life! They have entered a beautiful paradise. They are met there by the other "children" and friends of Narnia now grown up: Polly and Digory, Peter, Edmund, and Lucy. Suddenly Aslan appears in all his glory. Standing in the Stable Door, he calls for the end of time—the final destruction of the world that was Narnia. The stars fall from the sky, the sun and moon turn to blood, and earthquakes and floods ravage the land (compare Joel 2:30-31). All of Narnia's inhabitants now come before Aslan to be judged. Some turn to his left and disappear into darkness and oblivion, while others turn to his right and enter paradise with Tirian and the children (compare Matthew 25:31-46).

When all is done, Aslan calls his creatures to "Come further up, come further in!" They have not even begun to comprehend what is before them. "No eye has seen, no ear has heard, no mind has conceived what God has prepared for those who love him" (1 Corinthians 2:9). As they follow Aslan to the heart of his country, the friends of Narnia make a startling discovery. This new country is strangely familiar. In fact, it is just like Narnia—only better! Lord Digory is the first to grasp the situation: The world they knew "was not the real Narnia. That had a beginning and an end. It was only a shadow or a copy of the real Narnia which has always been here and always will be here. . . . You need not mourn over Narnia, Lucy. All of the old Narnia that mattered, all the dear creatures, have been drawn into the real Narnia through the Door."

Their old friends are gathered there waiting for them—kings and queens and heroes of the faith—those who had gone on before. In the midst of their joyous reunion, Lucy has only one fear—that Aslan will once again send her and the others back to their own world. But this time there is no going back. Aslan explains that the "terrible jerk" that brought them all into Narnia was a railway accident. "Have you not guessed? . . . You are—as you used to call it in the Shadowlands—dead. The term is over: the holidays have begun!"

And so they discover that "All their life in this world and all their adventures in Narnia had only been the cover and the title page. Now at last they were beginning Chapter One of the Great Story which no one on earth has read: which goes on forever: in which every chapter is better than the last."

What a glorious picture of the true destiny of all believers! This and much more will you discover as you join King Tirian for *The Last Battle*.

1. BY CALDRON POOL

But I am afraid that just as Eve was deceived by the serpent's cunning, your minds may somehow be led astray from your sincere and pure devotion to Christ. 2 CORINTHIANS 11:3

Biblical Parallels and Principles

Shift claims to be Puzzle's friend, but he treats the donkey more like a servant—taking the best of everything for himself. The Scripture tells us, "No one should wrong his brother or take advantage of him" (1 Thessalonians 4:6). Instead, Galatians 5:13 says, "Serve one another in love." And Romans 12:10 says, "Honor one another above yourselves."

Shift is a master manipulator. He convinces Puzzle that by pretending to be Aslan, he will have a chance to "set everything right in Narnia." The only thing Shift is truly interested in is gratifying his own lusts. Of such people the apostle Paul said, "Their destiny is destruction, their god is their stomach, and their glory is in their shame. Their mind is on earthly things" (Philippians 3:19). God is not deceived. "The LORD searches every heart and understands every motive behind the thoughts" (1 Chronicles 28:9).

Think About It!

As Chapter One begins, we're told that this story takes place in "the last days of Narnia." Shift and Puzzle are thrown on their faces by a small earthquake. What signs does the Bible say will signal the last days of Earth?

(Hint: Read Mark 13:7-8.)

Scriptures on Reverence for God

Psalm 99:1-3   Deuteronomy 13:4   Psalm 111:10

2. THE RASHNESS OF THE KING

"Watch out that no one deceives you. Many will come in my name, claiming, 'I am he,' and will deceive many." MARK 13:5-6

Biblical Parallels and Principles

🕉 Roonwit says that if Aslan had truly come, "the sky would have foretold it." Amos 3:7 tells us, "Surely the Sovereign LORD does nothing without revealing his plan to his servants the prophets."

🕉 None of the Narnians have firsthand knowledge of Aslan—they only remember the old stories. All they seem to understand about his nature is that "He is not a tame lion." The Scripture tells us that God is indeed all-powerful—He cannot be controlled or manipulated. But He is also good and just and kind. "The LORD is righteous in all his ways and loving toward all he has made" (Psalm 145:17).

🕉 When the King sees a Talking Horse being beaten, he reacts with fury, killing its Calormene slave drivers. This scene is nearly identical to the one in Exodus 2:11-12, where Moses comes upon an Egyptian beating a Hebrew slave. In his anger, Moses rashly murders the Egyptian. When his actions become known, he must flee from his palace home to the desert of Midian.

Do You Know?

The Centaur urges King Tirian not to act immediately—he should wait for reinforcements. But in his wrath, Tirian refuses to listen to wise counsel. According to the Bible, what does a quick-tempered man lack?

(Hint: Read Proverbs 14:7.)

Scriptures on Recklessness and Restraint

Proverbs 14:16   Proverbs 17:27   1 Peter 4:7

3. THE APE IN ITS GLORY

Do not believe every spirit, but test the spirits to see whether they are from God, because many false prophets have gone out into the world. 1 JOHN 4:1

Biblical Parallels and Principles

❧ After murdering the Calormene slave drivers, Tirian and Jewel flee—just as Moses fled after he killed the Egyptian in Exodus 2:11-12.

❧ The King and the Unicorn can't believe the reports of Aslan's cruelty and injustice. At the same time, they can't help but wonder if they have been mistaken in their faith in him. The Scripture is clear that God never changes (Malachi 3:6). He is "righteous in all his ways and loving toward all he has made" (Psalm 145:17). "Let God be true, and every man a liar" (Romans 3:4). "If we are faithless, he will remain faithful, for he cannot disown himself" (2 Timothy 2:13).

❧ The Narnians are confused by Shift's charade. They don't know what to believe. In Mark 13:22-23, Jesus warned His disciples, "False Christs and false prophets will appear and perform signs and miracles to deceive the elect. . . . So be on your guard." Second Peter 2:1-3 says, "They will secretly introduce destructive heresies. . . . Many will follow their shameful ways. . . . In their greed these teachers will exploit you with stories they have made up." Second John 7 explains, "Any such person is the deceiver and the antichrist."

❧ The squirrels are ordered to deliver more nuts—"twice as many . . . by sunset tomorrow . . . or, my word! you'll catch it." When the Israelites were in bondage to Egypt, the slave drivers forced them to make bricks and meet certain quotas. When Moses spoke up to Pharaoh, he retaliated by withholding straw. Their work was in effect doubled (Exodus 5:1-19).

❧ Shift says there will be no more crowding around Aslan—though in the old days Aslan clearly welcomed the creatures to gather around him. (See *The Lion, the Witch and the Wardrobe* and *Prince Caspian*.) Jesus called the crowds to Him (Matthew 9:36; 15:10). When His disciples tried to keep people from bothering Him with their babies, He told them, "Let the little children come to me, and do not hinder them" (Luke 18:16).

❧ The Ape says that though Aslan used to speak to the Talking Beasts face to face, He will now speak only through Shift, his "mouthpiece." Scripture tells us the exact opposite is true of God. "In the past God spoke to our forefathers through the prophets at many times and in various ways, but in these last days he has spoken to us by his Son" (Hebrews 1:1-2).

❧ The Lamb asks, "What have we to do with the Calormenes?" And it is the best question asked so far. Second Corinthians 6:14-16 says, "Do not be yoked together with unbelievers. For what do righteousness and wickedness have in common? Or what fellowship can light have with darkness? What harmony is there between Christ and Belial? . . . What agreement is there between the temple of God and idols?"

❧ Tirian is distressed at how quickly and easily his subjects are deceived. The apostle Paul had the same frustration with believers in Corinth: "If someone comes to you and preaches a Jesus other than the Jesus we preached . . . or a different gospel from the one you accepted, you put up with it easily enough. . . . For such men are false apostles, deceitful work-men, masquerading as apostles of Christ. And no wonder, for Satan him-self masquerades as an angel of light" (2 Corinthians 11:4, 13-14).

❧ Tirian reflects on the nature of "the good Lion by whose blood all Narnia was saved." The Bible tells us that we are all saved by Christ's atoning work on the cross. "In him we have redemption through his blood" (Ephesians 1:7; see also Colossians 1:19-20; Revelation 1:5).

Do You Know?

The Ape announces that times have changed. Aslan will no longer be merciful and loving and kind. "He's going to lick you into shape this time!" Has Aslan really changed? What does the Bible tell us about the nature of God?

(Hint: Read Malachi 3:6 and Hebrews 13:8.)

Scriptures on the Coming of the Antichrist
2 John 7   1 John 2:18, 22   1 John 4:1-3

4. WHAT HAPPENED THAT NIGHT

Friend deceives friend, and no one speaks the truth. They have taught their tongues to lie; they wear themselves out with sinning. You live in the midst of deception. JEREMIAH 9:5-6

Biblical Parallels and Principles

࿇ The creatures have gathered around the Stable to catch a glimpse of Aslan. They are deceived by Shift and Puzzle's masquerade. Jesus warned His disciples, "At that time if anyone says to you, 'Look, here is the Christ!' or, 'There he is!' do not believe it. For false Christs and false prophets will appear and perform great signs and miracles to deceive even the elect—if that were possible. . . . So if anyone tells you, 'There he is, out in the desert,' do not go out; or, 'Here he is, in the inner rooms,' do not believe it. For as lightning that comes from the east is visible even in the west, so will be the coming of the Son of Man" (Matthew 24:23-27).

࿇ The Talking Beasts cry out in distress, "Aslan! Speak to us! Comfort us. Be angry with us no more." The Scripture records many occasions when God's people voiced those same words. The psalmist prayed, "Do not hide your face from me, do not turn your servant away in anger. . . . Do not reject me or forsake me" (Psalm 27:9). "Restore us again, O God our Savior, and put away your displeasure toward us. . . . Show us your unfailing love" (Psalm 85:4, 7).

࿇ When he cries out for help, Tirian appears to the Seven Friends of Narnia as a ghost or vision. Compare this scene to Acts 16:9-10: "During the night Paul had a vision of a man of Macedonia standing and begging him, 'Come over to Macedonia and help us' . . . we got ready at once to leave for Macedonia, concluding that God had called us to preach the gospel to them."

Think About It!

King Tirian remembers how Aslan and the children from another world always came to Narnia "when things were at their worst." As dark as it is, he begins to hope. What did the psalmist do in his dark moments?

(Hint: Read Psalm 77:1-14.)

Scriptures on God's Answer to Our Cry for Help

Psalm 34:4-8   Isaiah 30:19   1 John 5:14-15

5. HOW HELP CAME TO THE KING

*The LORD is near to all who call on him, to all who call on him
in truth. He fulfills the desires of those who fear him; he hears
their cry and saves them.* PSALM 145:18-19

Biblical Parallels and Principles

⚜ The Seven Friends of Narnia respond immediately to the vision of
Tirian, just as the apostles responded to the vision of the man of
Macedonia. "We got ready at once . . . concluding that God had called us"
(Acts 16:10). Ephesians 5:15-17 tells believers, "Be very careful, then,
how you live—not as unwise but as wise, making the most of every
opportunity, because the days are evil . . . understand what the Lord's will
is." Galatians 6:10 adds, "As we have opportunity, let us do good to all
people, especially those who belong to the family of believers."

⚜ Tirian now acts with caution and forethought. Proverbs 27:12 says, "The
prudent see danger and take refuge, but the simple keep going and suffer
for it." Proverbs 14:15 observes that "a prudent man gives thought to his
steps." And 1 Peter 4:7 warns, "The end of all things is near. Therefore be
clear minded and self-controlled."

Do You Know?

Tirian and the children escape to a fortified tower that the King's ancestors
built for use in times of trouble. According to the Bible, where do the righteous find refuge?

(Hint: Read Proverbs 18:10.)

Scriptures on God's Timing

Ecclesiastes 3:1-8, 11   2 Peter 3:8-9   Galatians 6:9

6. A GOOD NIGHT'S WORK

We will no longer be infants, tossed back and forth by the waves,
and blown here and there by every wind of teaching and by the
cunning and craftiness of men in their deceitful scheming.

EPHESIANS 4:14

Biblical Parallels and Principles

Narnia is silent; gloom and fear reigns over the land. The Bible tells us that a day is coming for our world when people "will look toward the earth and see only distress and darkness and fearful gloom" (Isaiah 8:22). God will bring judgment on those who have profaned His name. "I will bring an end to the sounds of joy and gladness . . . the land will become desolate" (Jeremiah 7:34).

Tirian would execute Puzzle on the spot, but Jill pleads with the King to show mercy. While the Scripture is clear that all of us are responsible for our own actions (James 1:13-15; Romans 3:10-11, 23), the Bible also tells us to be merciful to those who are easily deceived and led astray. "We who are strong ought to bear with the failings of the weak" (Romans 15:1; see also Psalm 41:1; Romans 14:1; 1 Thessalonians 5:14). Those who take advantage of the simple-hearted will experience God's wrath: "If anyone causes one of these little ones who believe in me to sin, it would be better for him to have a large millstone hung around his neck and to be drowned in the depths of the sea" (Matthew 18:6).

Think About It!

Tirian decides to meet the approaching dwarfs and reveal Shift's deception to them. How does the Bible say believers should react to wicked schemes?

(Hint: Read Ephesians 5:8-12.)

Scriptures on the Night

John 9:4   Romans 13:11-12   1 Thessalonians 5:1-8

7. MAINLY ABOUT DWARFS

Furthermore, since they did not think it worthwhile to retain the knowledge of God, he gave them over to a depraved mind, to do what ought not to be done. ROMANS 1:28

Biblical Parallels and Principles

⚹ Tirian announces, "The light is dawning, the lie broken." Romans 13:11-13 tells true believers, "The hour has come for you to wake up from your slumber, because our salvation is nearer now than when we first believed. The night is nearly over; the day is almost here. So let us put aside the deeds of darkness and put on the armor of light."

⚹ The Dwarfs refuse to believe in the one true Aslan. They taunt Tirian and the children and demand proof of Aslan's existence. In Jesus' day, the religious leaders taunted Him the same way: "What miraculous sign can you show us to prove your authority to do all this?" (John 2:18; see also Matthew 16:1; Luke 11:16; John 7:4-5).

⚹ Ginger is revealed as the instigator of the Dwarfs' rebellion and the author of many of the lies told to the other Talking Beasts. First John 2:22 asks, "Who is the liar? It is the man who denies that Jesus is the Christ. Such a man is the antichrist—he denies the Father and the Son." Second Peter 2:3, 10-13 says, "In their greed these teachers will exploit you with stories they have made up. . . . Bold and arrogant, these men are not afraid to slander celestial beings . . . these men blaspheme in matters they do not understand. They are like brute beasts . . . and like beasts they too will perish. They will be paid back with harm for the harm they have done."

Sound Familiar?

Poggin is the only dwarf to come back and show gratitude to Tirian for his rescue. The Bible tells us Jesus rescued ten men from something terrible, but only one of them came back to say thank you. Do you remember what Jesus had rescued him from?

(Hint: Read Luke 17:11-19.)

Scriptures on Those Who Plot Evil

Proverbs 16:27-30   Proverbs 6:12-15   Isaiah 32:7-8

8. WHAT NEWS THE EAGLE BROUGHT

But mark this: There will be terrible times in the last days.

2 TIMOTHY 3:1

Biblical Parallels and Principles

☙ Poggin observes that "people shouldn't call for demons unless they really mean what they say." The Bible tells us that demons and evil spirits really do exist. While believers should be aware of and alert to their activities, we have no need to fear them (1 John 4:4). But unbelievers had better beware. They don't know who they are dealing with. "Some Jews who went around driving out evil spirits tried to invoke the name of the Lord Jesus over those who were demon-possessed. They would say, 'In the name of Jesus, whom Paul preaches, I command you to come out.' . . . One day the evil spirit answered them, 'Jesus I know, and I know about Paul, but who are you?' Then the man who had the evil spirit jumped on them and overpowered them all. He gave them such a beating that they ran out of the house naked and bleeding" (Acts 19:13-15).

☙ Jewel was about to be executed for refusing to worship the false Aslan. The Bible tells us, "Everyone who wants to live a godly life in Christ Jesus will be persecuted, while evil men and impostors will go from bad to worse, deceiving and being deceived" (2 Timothy 3:12-13). In the end times a hideous "beast" will rule the world, causing "all who refused to worship the image to be killed" (Revelation 13:15). Jesus told His disciples that some of them would be persecuted, betrayed, and even put to death: "All men will hate you because of me. But . . . by standing firm you will gain life" (Luke 21:17-19).

☙ Roonwit says a noble death is a treasure that no one is too poor to buy. The Bible tells us, "Precious in the sight of the LORD is the death of his saints" (Psalm 116:15). "Blessed is the man who perseveres under trial, because when he has stood the test, he will receive the crown of life that God has promised to those who love him" (James 1:12).

Do You Know?

Jewel tells Jill that all worlds come to an end except Aslan's country. What does the Bible tell us will happen to our world?

(Hint: Read 2 Peter 3:10 and Revelation 21:1-5.)

Scriptures on the Existence and Activity of Evil Spirits

John 8:44   Ephesians 6:12   1 Timothy 4:1

9. THE GREAT MEETING ON STABLE HILL

Then the LORD said to me, "The prophets are prophesying lies in my name. I have not sent them or appointed them or spoken to them. They are prophesying to you false visions, divinations, idolatries and the delusions of their own minds." JEREMIAH 14:14

Biblical Parallels and Principles

Jewel says there is nothing to do but "go back to Stable Hill, proclaim the truth, and take the adventure that Aslan sends us." The Bible tells us that believers are called to be a light in the darkness (Matthew 5:14). "The time will come when men will not put up with sound doctrine. . . . They will turn their ears away from the truth and turn aside to myths" (2 Timothy 4:3-4). Jesus said we are His witnesses (Acts 1:8), charged with proclaiming the truth (Romans 10:8-10; 1 John 1:3-5). "Be faithful, even to the point of death, and I will give you the crown of life" (Revelation 2:10).

Jewel and King Tirian are certain that death awaits them, yet they remain resolute. The apostle Paul told fellow Christians, "We are hard pressed on every side, but not crushed; perplexed, but not in despair; persecuted, but not abandoned; struck down, but not destroyed. We always carry around in our body the death of Jesus, so that the life of Jesus may also be revealed in our body. For we who are alive are always being given over to death for Jesus' sake . . . we know that the one who raised the Lord Jesus from the dead will also raise us. . . . Therefore we do not lose heart. . . . For our light and momentary troubles are achieving for us an eternal glory that far outweighs them all" (2 Corinthians 4:8-17).

Think About It!

By mixing in a little truth, Rishda and Shift make their lie stronger. According to the Bible, who was the first person to use this strategy to deceive God's people?

(Hint: Read Genesis 3:1-6.)

Scriptures on Facing Death Without Fear

Romans 14:8   Philippians 1:21   1 Corinthians 15:55-58

10. WHO WILL GO INTO
THE STABLE?

Let the wicked be put to shame. . . . Let their lying lips be
silenced. PSALM 31:17-18

Biblical Parallels and Principles

While the Dwarfs are right to be skeptical of Rishda's claims, their asser-
tion that "seeing is believing" could not be more wrong. Second
Corinthians 5:7 says, "We live by faith, not by sight." While Jesus did
many signs and wonders during His earthly ministry, He refused to "perform" for the rebellious, unbelieving people who demanded a sign as
proof of His divine authority. To doubting Thomas, Jesus said, "Because
you have seen me, you have believed; blessed are those who have not seen
and yet have believed" (John 20:29).

King Tirian says to Jill, "Courage, child: we are all between the paws of
the true Aslan." The psalmist prayed, "Into your hands I commit my
spirit" (Psalm 31:5). Deuteronomy 33:27 tells us, "The eternal God is
your refuge, and underneath are the everlasting arms." Romans 14:8
reminds us, "If we live, we live to the Lord; and if we die, we die to the
Lord. So whether we live or die, we belong to the Lord."

Rishda knows that he is sending Emeth to his death. He cannot dis-
suade him, and he will not jeopardize his position by revealing the
truth. He echoes the words of Pontius Pilate in Matthew 27:24. Pilate
did not want to send Jesus to His death, but he lacked moral courage.
He put the decision on the crowd, washed his hands in front of them,
and announced, "I am innocent of this man's blood."

The Narnian creatures are terrified of Tashlan and beg Shift to speak to
him on their behalf. Although the context is completely different, the
imagery in this scene comes right out of Exodus 19—20. "Mount Sinai
was covered with smoke . . . the whole mountain trembled violently. . . .
When the people saw the thunder and lightning and heard the trumpet
and saw the mountain in smoke, they trembled with fear. They stayed at
a distance and said to Moses, 'Speak to us yourself and we will listen. But
do not have God speak to us or we will die'" (19:18; 20:18-19).

Do You Know?

Ginger, who invented many of the lies about Aslan, suddenly loses his ability to speak. He ceases to be a Talking Beast. The Bible tells us about a wicked man named Elymas who tried to deceive people and turn them away from God. Do you know what happened to him?

(Hint: Read Acts 13:9-11.)

Scriptures on Living by Faith

1 Peter 1:8-9   1 Corinthians 16:13   Hebrews 11

11. THE PACE QUICKENS

The wrath of God is being revealed from heaven against all the godlessness and wickedness of men who suppress the truth.

ROMANS 1:18

Biblical Parallels and Principles

The lines have been drawn, and the last battle of Narnia has begun. Speaking of the end of our world, Jesus said, "Nation will rise against nation, and kingdom against kingdom. There will be famines and earthquakes . . . you will be handed over to be persecuted and put to death, and you will be hated by all nations because of me . . . many will turn away from the faith and will betray and hate each other, and many false prophets will appear and deceive many people. Because of the increase of wickedness, the love of most will grow cold, but he who stands firm to the end will be saved" (Matthew 24:7-13).

The end has come. King Tirian and the others are fighting a battle they know they cannot win. The apostle Peter responded to questions from believers who didn't know what to do in such a hopeless situation. "Since everything will be destroyed in this way, what kind of people ought you to be? You ought to live holy and godly lives as you look forward to the day of God and speed its coming. That day will bring about the destruction of the heavens by fire, and the elements will melt in the heat. But in keeping with his promise we are looking forward to a new heaven and a new earth, the home of righteousness. So . . . make every effort to be found spotless, blameless and at peace with him" (2 Peter 3:11-14).

Do You Know?

Rishda has called on gods he does not believe in—and it seems they have come. What does the Bible say will happen to men like him?

(Hint: Read 1 Timothy 1:20 and 2 Thessalonians 1:8-9.)

Scriptures on Fighting the Good Fight

1 Timothy 6:12-16   Ephesians 6:10-18   Hebrews 12:1-3

12. THROUGH THE STABLE DOOR

*The Lord will rescue me from every evil attack and bring me
safely to his heavenly kingdom.* 2 TIMOTHY 4:18

Biblical Parallels and Principles

⚛ Jewel tells Jill that they may very well be about to enter Aslan's country
(by death), "and we shall sup at his table tonight." The Scripture tells us
that for believers, death is merely the doorway to Heaven. Jesus told the
thief on the cross next to Him, "Today you will be with me in paradise"
(Luke 23:43). Many Scriptures speak of Heaven as a banquet or feast (for
example, Psalm 23:5-6; Matthew 22:2-14; Luke 14:16-24; Revelation
3:20). "Blessed are those who are invited to the wedding supper of the
Lamb" (Revelation 19:9).

⚛ Peter rebukes Tash in the name of Aslan. He says that Tash can take Rishda,
who belongs to him, but he cannot lay a hand on Tirian. In John 8:44 Jesus
referred to blasphemers as children of the devil—they belong to Satan. But
Satan has no power over the children of God. We have been redeemed by
the blood of Jesus (1 Peter 1:18-19; Revelation 5:9). Jesus said that all
authority in Heaven and earth had been given to Him (Matthew 28:18).
He gave this authority to His disciples in Mark 16:17: "In my name they
will drive out demons." (See Luke 10:17 and the book of Acts for more
examples.)

Can That Be Right?

Peter says that Susan is "no longer a friend of Narnia." Over the years many
Christians have argued over whether C.S. Lewis meant that Susan had forever
forsaken her faith (and would thus be doomed to Hell) or whether she was
merely backslidden. In at least one letter to a child who wrote to ask about it,
Lewis hinted that Susan's defection might well be permanent. However, he
added that since she is left living at the end of *The Chronicles*, "there is plenty of
time for her to mend, and perhaps she will get to Aslan's country in the end—
in her own way."

Scriptures on True Maturity

2 Peter 1:5-11   Ephesians 4:11-16   James 1:2-4

13. HOW THE DWARFS REFUSE TO BE TAKEN IN

"O Jerusalem, Jerusalem, you who kill the prophets and stone those sent to you, how often I have longed to gather your children together, as a hen gathers her chicks under her wings, but you were not willing!" LUKE 13:34

Biblical Parallels and Principles

❧ Aslan's country is full of luscious fruit trees. The Bible tells us there will be such trees in Heaven: "On each side of the river stood the tree of life, bearing twelve crops of fruit, yielding its fruit every month. And the leaves of the tree are for the healing of the nations" (Revelation 22:2).

❧ Aslan cannot help the Dwarfs: "They will not let us help them. . . . Their prison is only in their minds, yet they are in that prison; and so afraid of being taken in that they cannot be taken out." Jesus wept over the city of Jerusalem and its unbelief (Luke 13:34; 19:41-42). "'Though seeing, they do not see; though hearing, they do not hear or understand. . . . For this people's heart has become calloused; they hardly hear with their ears, and they have closed their eyes. Otherwise they might see with their eyes, hear with their ears, understand with their hearts and turn, and I would heal them'" (Matthew 13:13-15).

❧ Tirian has been faithful to the bitter end. Now, instead of a miserable stable, he finds himself in Paradise—dressed in royal robes and in the company of the Seven Friends of Narnia. As the apostle Paul awaited execution, he reflected, "I have fought the good fight, I have finished the race, I have kept the faith. Now there is in store for me the crown of righteousness, which the Lord, the righteous Judge, will award to me on that day—and not only to me, but also to all who have longed for his appearing" (2 Timothy 4:7-8).

❧ Aslan greets Tirian: "Well done, last of the Kings of Narnia who stood firm at the darkest hour." He echoes the words Jesus used to describe how God will respond to the obedience of His people: "Well done, good and faithful servant!" (Matthew 25:21). Jesus told His disciples, "He who stands firm to the end will be saved" (Mark 13:13; see also Luke 21:19; Philippians 1:27; Colossians 1:23; 2 Thessalonians 2:15).

Think About It!

Lucy says, "In our world too, a stable once had something inside it that was bigger than our whole world." Do you know what she means?

(Hint: Read Luke 2:1-20.)

Scriptures on Our Heart's Desire

Psalm 84:1-2, 10   Isaiah 26:8   Philippians 3:7-11

14. NIGHT FALLS ON NARNIA

The Lord's coming is near. . . . The Judge is standing at the door!
JAMES 5:8-9

Biblical Parallels and Principles

⛬ At Aslan's command, Father Time blows his horn to signal the end of the world. Matthew 24:30-31 tells us that when our world comes to an end, "The Son of Man will appear. . . . And he will send his angels with a loud trumpet call, and they will gather his elect from the four winds, from one end of the heavens to the other." (See also 1 Corinthians 15:52; 1 Thessalonians 4:16; Revelation 8:2.)

⛬ The Narnian stars begin to fall from the sky. Joel 3:15 tells us that on the Day of the Lord, "the sun and moon will be darkened, and the stars no longer shine." Mark 13:25 says, "The stars will fall from the sky, and the heavenly bodies will be shaken." (See also Matthew 24:29; Luke 21:25.)

⛬ The creatures look straight into Aslan's face. They then turn to the left (darkness and oblivion) or to the right (Paradise). Matthew 25:31-33 says, "When the Son of Man comes in his glory, and all the angels with him, he will sit on his throne in heavenly glory. All the nations will be gathered before him, and he will separate the people one from another as a shepherd separates the sheep from the goats. He will put the sheep on his right and the goats on his left." Those on the left will "go away to eternal punishment, but the righteous to eternal life" (v. 46).

⛬ Narnia is laid bare. The book of Revelation describes the wars, plagues, and famines that will one day decimate the earth. (Not to mention the destruction brought on by the Antichrist and the Beast.) Second Peter 3:10 says, "The heavens will disappear with a roar; the elements will be destroyed by fire, and the earth and everything in it will be laid bare." (See also Luke 21:25.)

⛬ Narnia's sun and moon turn red as they die. Joel 2:31 says that on the great and dreadful Day of the Lord, "The sun will be turned to darkness and the moon to blood." Revelation 6:12 says, "The sun turned black . . . the whole moon turned blood red."

Do You Know?

Aslan calls the High King Peter to close the door. Peter locks it with a golden key. In the Bible, Jesus said He held "the keys of death and Hades" (Revelation 1:18). And He told one of His disciples that He would give them "the keys of the kingdom of heaven." Do you know which disciple He was speaking to?

(Hint: Read Matthew 16:18-19.)

Scriptures on the Coming Judgment

2 Corinthians 5:10   Romans 2:5-11, 16   Revelation 20:12-13

15. FURTHER UP AND FURTHER IN

"Blessed are the pure in heart, for they will see God."

MATTHEW 5:8

Biblical Parallels and Principles

᷂ Without realizing it, Emeth has been seeking and serving Aslan all of his life. ("Emeth" is a Hebrew word for "faithful" or "true.") Acts 10:35 tells us that God "accepts men from every nation who fear him and do what is right." Emeth shares the passion of the psalmist who said, "I am a stranger to my brothers . . . for zeal for your house consumes me" (Psalm 69:8-9). "Your face, LORD, I will seek" (Psalm 27:8). "I seek you with all my heart" (Psalm 119:10). God always responds to those who earnestly desire the truth. (See the story of the Ethiopian in Acts 8:26-39.)

᷂ Compare Emeth's description of Aslan to John's description of Jesus in Revelation 1:14-17: "His head and hair were white like wool, as white as snow, and his eyes were like a blazing fire. His feet were like bronze glowing in a furnace, and his voice was like the sound of rushing waters. . . . His face was like the sun shining in all its brilliance. When I saw him I fell at his feet as though dead. Then he placed his right hand on me and said, 'Do not be afraid.'"

᷂ Aslan breathed on Emeth, taking away his fear. In John 20:21-22 Jesus appeared to His frightened disciples and said, "'Peace be with you!' . . . And with that he breathed on them."

᷂ Lord Digory explains that the old Narnia was only "a shadow or a copy of the real Narnia." Colossians 2:17 tells us that everything that came before Jesus was merely "a shadow of the things that were to come; the reality, however, is found in Christ." The sanctuary that Moses built was "a copy and shadow of what is in heaven" (Hebrews 8:5). The Law itself is "only a shadow of the good things that are coming—not the realities themselves" (Hebrews 10:1). God will one day create a new heaven and a new earth. "There will be no more death or mourning or crying or pain, for the old order of things has passed away" (Revelation 21:4).

Can That Be Right?

Some readers have wondered if Emeth is C.S. Lewis's way of saying that all religions lead to the one true God and that anyone who is sincere in their beliefs will find their way to Heaven. Nothing could be further from the truth. (Note how Aslan responded to Emeth's question as to whether he and Tash were one and the same after all.) We know that C.S. Lewis believed that faith in Jesus Christ is the only way that anyone can be saved. (See John 14:6.) The character of Emeth illustrates the truth of Jeremiah 29:13: "You will seek me and find me when you seek me with all your heart." God is so merciful—He reveals Himself to those who truly seek Him, even if they are coming at it from the wrong direction. That was certainly Lewis's experience when he met God after thirty years as an atheist.

Scriptures on Seeking and Finding

Matthew 7:7-8   Psalm 105:3   Proverbs 8:17, 35

16. FAREWELL TO SHADOWLANDS

No eye has seen, no ear has heard, no mind has conceived what
God has prepared for those who love him. 1 CORINTHIANS 2:9

Biblical Parallels and Principles

❧ The friends realize that no matter what they do, they are not hot or tired or out of breath. They also cannot feel fear. Revelation 21:3-4 tells us how different Heaven will be from our experience in this life: "Now the dwelling of God is with men, and he will live with them. They will be his people, and God himself will be with them and be their God. He will wipe every tear from their eyes. There will be no more death or mourning or crying or pain, for the old order of things has passed away." Revelation 22:4-5 adds, "They will see his face. . . . There will be no more night."

❧ The call to go "further up and further in" is one that we can heed on earth as well as in Heaven. In Philippians 3:13-14 the apostle Paul said, "Forgetting what is behind and straining toward what is ahead, I press on toward the goal to win the prize for which God has called me heavenward." Hebrews 12:1-2 says, "Therefore, since we are surrounded by such a great cloud of witnesses, let us throw off everything that hinders and the sin that so easily entangles, and let us run with perseverance the race marked out for us. Let us fix our eyes on Jesus, the author and perfecter of our faith."

❧ The Kings and Queens join a joyful procession following Aslan further and deeper into his glorious country. The Bible says this is the destiny of all true believers. "You are a chosen people, a royal priesthood, a holy nation, a people belonging to God, that you may declare the praises of him who called you out of darkness into his wonderful light" (1 Peter 2:9). "Thanks be to God, who always leads us in triumphal procession in Christ and through us spreads everywhere the fragrance of the knowledge of him" (2 Corinthians 2:14). "We will also reign with him" (2 Timothy 2:12), "for ever and ever" (Revelation 22:5).

Think About It!

The friends discover that "everyone you had ever heard of"—all "the great heroes of Narnia"—await them in Aslan's country. The Bible tells us that we have "a great cloud of witnesses" cheering us on in our race of faith. They wait to welcome us into Heaven. Can you name some of these heroes of our faith?

(Hint: Read Hebrews 11:1-40; 12:1.)

Scriptures on Pressing in and Pressing on

1 Corinthians 9:24-27   Ephesians 3:14-21   Revelation 22:12-13

Epilogue

In *The Last Battle*, the final book in *The Chronicles of Narnia*, Peter and Lucy and the others are very confused. They have just witnessed the complete destruction of Narnia, and yet they now find themselves in a land very like it—only better! Lord Digory is the first one to grasp the situation:

> "Listen, Peter. When Aslan said you could never go back to Narnia, he meant the Narnia you were thinking of. But that was not the real Narnia. That had a beginning and an end. It was only a shadow or a copy of the real Narnia which has always been here and always will be here. . . . You need not mourn over Narnia, Lucy. All of the old Narnia that mattered, all the dear creatures, have been drawn into the real Narnia through the Door."

> It was the Unicorn who summed up what everyone was feeling. He stamped his right forefoot on the ground and neighed and then cried, "I have come home at last! This is my real country! I belong here. This is the land I have been looking for all of my life, though I never knew it till now. The reason why we loved the old Narnia is that it sometimes looked a little like this. Bree-hee-hee! Come further up, come further in!"

At the Unicorn's call, the Seven Kings and Queens and their friends begin running deeper and deeper into the country. But no matter how far they go, they find that there is always more ahead. And over and over the call is heard, "Further up and further in!"

> All their life in this world and all their adventures in Narnia had only been the cover and the title page. Now at last they were beginning Chapter One of the Great Story which no one on earth has read: which goes on forever: in which every chapter is better than the last.

We live now in what C.S. Lewis called the "Shadowlands." Our life here on earth is but a pale copy—a faulty, imperfect imitation—of what is to come. And what we think of as the end (death) is really just the beginning.

"No eye has seen, no ear has heard, no mind has conceived what God has prepared for those who love him" (1 Corinthians 2:9).

In *The Voyage of the Dawn Treader* (Book 5 of *The Chronicles*), Aslan tells two of the Pevensies that their adventures in Narnia have come to an end. Both children are horribly upset.

> "It isn't Narnia, you know," sobbed Lucy. "It's you. We shan't meet you there. And how can we live, never meeting you?"
> "But you shall meet me, dear one," said Aslan.
> "Are—are you there too, Sir?" said Edmund.
> "I am," said Aslan. "But there I have another name. You must learn to know me by that name. This was the very reason why you were brought to Narnia, that by knowing me here for a little, you may know me better there."

Unlike life in the Shadowlands, our adventures in Heaven will never end. But our journey begins here and now. God gives us this time in the Shadowlands so that by knowing Him here for a little while, we may know Him better in eternity.

And the truth is, we will never get to the end of God. No matter how old we become, no matter how long we walk with Him, we will never run out of things to learn about Him. We will never know all there is to know. There will always be something more, something deeper, something truer than what we have yet experienced. "Call to me and I will answer you and tell you great and unsearchable things that you do not know" (Jeremiah 33:3).

As we grow in our faith, we grow in our capacity to know and understand who God is. We grow in our ability to receive what He has to give us. We grow in appreciation of all that He is and all that He has done for us.

My prayer is that with this guide to *The Chronicles of Narnia*—and the Word of God that inspired them—you have been encouraged and strengthened in your own personal journey of faith.

The more we learn, the richer and fuller and deeper our relationship with God becomes. And still He calls to us, "Come further up, come further in!"

In 1955 a nine-year-old boy named Laurence began reading *The Chronicles of Narnia*. He grew very concerned because, as he confessed to his mother, he felt that he loved Aslan more than Jesus. He was terribly afraid that this made him an "idol-worshipper." Laurence's mother didn't know quite what to say; so she wrote a letter to C.S. Lewis, care of his publisher, to ask for his advice. Ten days later she received the following reply:

Dear Mrs. K,

Tell Laurence from me, with my love:

1) Even if he was loving Aslan more than Jesus (I'll explain in a moment why he really can't be doing this) he would not be an idol-worshipper. If he was an idol-worshipper he'd be doing it on purpose, whereas he's now doing it because he can't help doing it, and trying hard not to do it. But God knows quite well how hard we find it to love Him more than anyone or anything else, and He won't be angry with us as long as we are trying. And He will help us.

2) But Laurence can't really love Aslan more than Jesus, even if he feels that's what he is doing. For the things he loves Aslan for doing or saying are simply things that Jesus really did and said. So that when Laurence thinks he is loving Aslan, he is really loving Jesus: and perhaps loving Him more than he ever did before. Of course there is one thing Aslan has that Jesus has not—I mean, the body of a lion. (But remember, if there are other worlds and they need to be saved and Christ were to save them as He would—He may really have taken all sorts of bodies in them which we don't know about.) Now if Laurence is bothered because he finds the lion-body seems nicer to him than the man-body, I don't think he need be bothered at all. God knows all about the way a little boy's imagination works (He made it, after all) and knows that at a certain age the idea of talking and friendly animals is very attractive. So I don't think He minds if Laurence likes the lion-body. And anyway, Laurence will find as he grows older, that feeling (liking the lion-body better) will die away of itself, without his taking any trouble about it. So he needn't bother.

3) If I were Laurence, I'd just say in my prayers something like this: "Dear God, if the things I've been thinking and feeling about those books are things You don't like and are bad for me, please take away those feelings and thoughts. But if they are not bad, then please stop me from worrying about them. And help me every day to love You more in the way that really matters far more than any feelings or imaginations, by doing what You want and growing more like You." That is the sort of thing I think Laurence should say for himself; but it would be kind and Christian-like if he then added, "And if Mr. Lewis has worried any other children by his books or done them any harm, then please forgive him and help him never to do it again."

Will this help? I am terribly sorry to have caused such trouble and would take it as a great favor if you would write again and tell me how Laurence goes on. I shall of course have him daily in my prayers. He must be a corker of a boy: I hope you are prepared for the possibility he might turn out a saint. I daresay the saints' mothers have, in some ways, a rough time!

Yours sincerely,
C.S. Lewis

Epilogue

There is no doubt that *The Chronicles Of Narnia* have influenced many a future "saint"—helping countless precious young people (and grown-ups too) to grasp some of the most profound truths of the Christian faith. And yes, many of us have—by loving Aslan—learned to love Jesus more than ever before.

Lewis kept up quite a correspondence. Over the years he answered dozens of letters from children who loved Narnia and wrote to ask him questions about the series. (They often enclosed drawings of their favorite characters and scenes.) "Why did Reepicheep do this?" "What did it mean when Aslan said that?" "When is the next book coming out?" A little less than a month before he died, Lewis wrote the following letter to a little girl named Ruth. Somehow his words seem a fond and fitting farewell to all of us, his devoted readers.

Dear Ruth,

Many thanks for your kind letter, and it was very good of you to write and tell me that you like my books; and what a very good letter you write for your age!

If you continue to love Jesus, nothing much can go wrong with you, and I hope that you may always do so. I'm so thankful that you realized the "hidden story" in the Narnian books. It is odd, children nearly *always* do, grown-ups hardly ever.

I'm afraid the Narnian series has come to an end, and am sorry to tell you that you can expect no more.

God bless you.

Yours sincerely,
C.S. Lewis

The text of Lewis's correspondence quoted here is taken from *C.S. Lewis: Letters to Children*, edited by Lyle W. Dorsett and Marjorie Lamp Mead (New York: Touchstone/Simon & Schuster, 1985).

RECOMMENDED RESOURCES

Dorsett, Lyle W. and Marjorie Lamp Mead. *C.S. Lewis: Letters to Children.* New York: Touchstone/Simon & Schuster, 1985.

Focus on the Family Radio Theatre, *The Chronicles Of Narnia.* An audio dramatization of each of the seven books in the series is available on cassette or compact disc, with an introduction by C.S. Lewis's stepson, Douglas Gresham. A production of Focus on the Family, in association with Tyndale House Publishers, Inc. For more information, call 1-800-A-FAMILY.

Ford, Paul F. *Companion to Narnia.* San Francisco: HarperCollins, 1994.

Lindskoog, Kathryn. *Journey into Narnia.* Pasadena, CA: Hope Publishing House, 1998.

Martindale, Wayne and Jerry Root. *The Quotable Lewis.* Wheaton, IL: Tyndale House, 1989.

Official website of *The Chronicles Of Narnia*: www.narnia.com.

Sibley, Brian. *The Land of Narnia.* San Francisco: HarperCollins, 1989.

SCRIPTURE INDEX